THEY WERE WAITING.
AND THEY WERE TIRED OF WAITING.
THEY WERE HUNGRY—
FOR A DECENT MEAL, FOR LOVE,
A REAL WOMAN, TO OPEN A BAR,
FOR THE FEEL AND THE SMELL OF HOME . . .

"The more I talk," Pop said, "the more I realize that we really want very little out of life. Just the simple things."

Macon smiled. "I believe that life can be broken down into four very simple things. A nice hot shower, a lusty meal, a good bowel movement, and a satisfactory sex life. If I could have those four things consistently I'd be a very happy man."

"You're a braggart," Pop laughed, "but it's a beautiful thought."

"And I want to operate one of those gurgling bathrooms again," Macon went on dreamily. "I think the next time I get to use a built-in, self-serving toilet I'll probably flush it dry. And, oh, to soak in a real, honest-to-goodness hot tub."

A plane passed overhead, guns hammering away. Macon went inside, undressed, and got into bed. He lit a cigarette and lay quietly, looking up into the darkness. "Maybe I'd want a house on top of a hill. What an odd thought," he said half aloud. "I'd like to open a house of ill repute on the top of a hill—that would scramble society's concepts no end. Having to look *up* at a whorehouse."

He laughed—because you had to laugh when you started to think that maybe you were going nuts. . . .

THE FINAL MISSION

By Mark Druck

ZEBRA BOOKS
KENSINGTON PUBLISHING CORP.

ZEBRA BOOKS

are published by

KENSINGTON PUBLISHING CORP.
21 East 40th Street
New York, N.Y. 10016

First Printing: September, 1978

CHAPTER I

The three men in the four-man tent were just getting ready for bed. Rush Macon was fixing his mosquito netting.

"I'm glad nobody in here is flying tomorrow," he said, without looking up from what he was doing. "If there's one thing I don't like it's when these operations jokers come clomping around in the middle of the night to wake someone up. It seems they never get the right guy until they have everybody else in the joint awake and cussin'."

He adjusted the netting on its two bamboo crossbars, one holding the net at the head of the bed and one supporting it at the bottom. He threw the netting down all around and stuck his head up inside like an encaged canary; he began tucking the bottom of the net under the inflated airmattress that made his narrow canvas cot look pregnant. The bottom of the netting disappeared quickly in this manner, finally leaving a small place on the side through which entrance could be attained. Macon took his heavy flying jacket off the nail above his bed, jammed it into his pillowcase, fluffed it tenderly, tossed the finished product onto the bed. From the strand of rope that extended from the bamboo crossbar at the foot of the bed to the side of the tent he took the single, somewhat soiled bed sheet, folded it lengthwise and placed it carefully on top of the folded olive-drab blanket that was already in place. He then gently pushed the pillow between the folds in the sheet and smoothed out the finished product with infinite affection.

Straightening up outside the netting he observed his handiwork studiously, yawned, shoving his hands up over his head. He stood slightly over six-feet, a little on the lean side, with brown hair cut so short it was impossible to tell if it was curly. His face had a summer resort tan and the whites of his eyes and teeth seemed to scream for attention, silencing a nose that was a little too long and a chin that receded slightly and quite ordinary, squinting eyes that disappeared into whispering crinkles playing about them.

Rogers, a small, blond pilot, dropped down on one of the two chairs in the center of the tent. He seemed annoyed, lit up a cigarette.

"I think I'll have to fly, Make," he told Macon. "Potts is going to be cancelled, according to operations. Since I'm the supernumerary, I'll fly."

"What's with Potts?" said Bruce Lloyd, the third man. He was lanky, dark, with a pleasant expression.

"I was just over at operations," Rogers said. "Brownie says Potts has malaria."

"Well, if one of those jokers wakes me," Macon snorted, "I'm going to commit all kinds of murder." He sat down in the other chair. "Things change around here faster than rabbits."

"Where are you going?" Lloyd said.

"We were briefed for shipping. Secondary is a bridge in Western Kyushu." Rogers uncrossed his leg, patted his knee nervously, recrossed the leg.

"A milk run," Macon said.

"They expect us to find a couple of DD's and DE's."

"Destroyer Escorts aren't too bad, but these destroyers are rough," Lloyd said. "You may have hardships there."

"Oh, well," Macon said, "just tell yourself you're going along for the experience." He chuckled to himself, fully content that he was being the life of the party.

A low, whining siren began to wail, interrupting any further thoughts he might have had on the subject. The three men moved mechanically out of the tent, gazed at the congested sky. Searchlights were playing and playfully chasing one another. In a nearby tent a radio gave bent to the transmitted conversations of the nightfighters who were tracking the Jap planes as they approached Okinawa.

"Pineapple four from Cocoanut two; Boggie at zero one eight degrees at four zero miles. Pineapple four from Cocoanut two; Boggie at zero one eight degrees at four zero miles. Out."

"We've got time for a weed in forty miles," Macon said and lit a cigarette. "I hope those AA jokers can do better than they did last night. It would be nice to see them hit something one time."

They walked to the revetment some fifty feet behind the tent, sat down with their backs to what remained of a stone wall, awaited the activities. The Japs had been sending two or three Bettys over every night in an effort to annoy the Americans,

7

keep them awake. Macon had blushingly admitted sleeping through the first two raids because there had been no one present to arouse him.

Lights about them began disappearing. The show seemed ready to begin.

"I'm glad the Nips don't have as many planes here as they had on Leyte," Bruce Lloyd said. "It made watching them difficult when you did it from the bottom of a foxhole."

"I'd certainly hate to be one of those Japs," Rogers said. "Coming over here alone or in pairs is no way to prepare for the future."

"Nuts," said Macon. "Twenty yen says these AA jokers don't even nudge them."

"You're on," Rogers said. "Sounds like a good bet. The law of averages says they've got to hit something."

"I don't think they've passed that law here," Macon said.

From the north came the sound of aircraft. The engines didn't belong to the AAF. The pitch was too high, undulations came too quickly and too softly.

Macon crushed his cigarette silently and watched the searchlights as they picked up the plane. The Jap was high—about 30,000 feet. The lights came from just about every part of the large island and the beams formed a cone as they converged on the intruder. The plane looked chalky white, since each new light that hit him made him look paler. He moved along slowly as if waiting cautiously for the guns to open up. Then they did!

Loud, flat thuds of the .90 mm guns to the north, the rapid coughing of the .37's that scattered popping balls of fire about the plane. It appeared as though everyone was hitting short and slightly behind.

The Jap was about 10 miles north of the area, still coming straight and level. Puffs of fire exploded near him and the .90's continued to thump, sounding like huge unseeen beasts beating their chests—but still the invader came on—heading straight for the strip. More heavy guns began to open up now. The battery behind the area fired once, paused to check its range and azimuth, then began in earnest. The battery across the way started, then came a half-dozen others. It sounded as though a corps of drunken bass drummers had gotten loose!

Macon was aware suddenly of the shouts of the men about him. Small groups in the trenches nearby were rooting the AA boys on and whenever another battery opened up a wave of chatter babbled through the area.

There, a burst just missed him! Groans and occasional yells; sounds resembling a baseball crowd's bemoaning the batter's having swung and missed! "Ohhhhh, close one . . ." "Get that meatball!" "Too low, too low, get up there, get it up!" "Well, let's go!" "Ten yen to the man who gets him!" "*Before* he drops his load; *before* . . ." "Just a wee bit higher, just a little—about 4,000 feet!" The noisy competition between the AA outfits and the catcalls of the men raised quite a din, even though there did seem to be an undercurrent of sound teasing the excitement of the chase. Keenly Macon wished for a cigarette.

Occasionally a burst would flash above the plane—there was one just behind it! It seemed to change its course now, perhaps it was climbing, but it was next to impossible to tell. The searchlights reestablished contact quickly. The Jap moved off course again, leaving the lights but they jumped over to him immediately. The batteries to the north slackened now and to the south some new ones began to bark. And still the invader came on!

"He *must* be on his bomb run," Lloyd said quickly. "He's right over the strip!"

The battery just over the hill to the north opened up again reluctantly—as if giving vent to one last desperate effort. But their salvo left the situation unaltered, so they quickly quit. The plane continued to plow on through the field of red-and-yellow poppies—it was absolutely uncanny to see him moving nonchalantly past all the bursts of flak with what seemed to be utter disregard for all the confusion he was causing. And, being so high, it naturally seemed as though he was going purposely slower than usual to tease his enemies.

Suddenly the shriek of another high-toned drone could be heard. This one was low, coming in from the north! He must have sneaked through the radar while everyone was getting excited about the plane at altitude. The swiftness and surprise of his arrival left everyone speechless. The AA boys were still firing at the first plane, spreading their pattern of fire among the stars. The low-flying Jap seemed to be beating his power settings to the firewall—he was wide-open! His engines screamed the attack as he came over the small, sharp hill to the north of the area. He popped into view no more than one-hundred feet above the tents, went soaring down the small valley toward the strip. He was over the area for a split second, but no one saw him there, actually not even those whose consuming curiosity kept their bellies out of the dirt. Then bombs were

10

exploding on the strip—the Jap had scored a direct hit! A fire started in one of the parking areas. As Macon picked himself out of the dirt it looked as though a couple of P-51's were burning. Trucks and men were moving there for there were other planes to be protected. Mounted blackout lights and muffled flashlights were rushing to the blaze.

The low-flying Jap had come, deposited his bomb load and left before anyone had realized what was happening!

"Wow!" cried a distant voice. In the whole area that was the only comment, and it seemed fully adequate.

The decoy, the high-flying craft, had moved south about ten miles. AA bursts still jumped about him and searchlights grilled him but he was still sailing nonchalantly along. The shock of the quick thrust had intensified speculation on the AA batteries' chances of bringing him down. Now voices were eager and terse. Suddenly there was a burst beside the plane. He swerved sharply to the west. The gunners, probably believing that they had hit him, stepped up their tempo. He was losing altitude quickly now, it was difficult for the searchlights to stay with him. The Jap passed the northwest coast of the island, which was only about a mile from the area, and headed out to sea. The gunners, blasting with heavies and cracking their automatic weapons, kept blazing away. The invader was either mortally wounded or was picking up extra speed in the dive. Only the searchlights to the west could reach him now and the distant batteries began quitting as their own beams gave up the pursuit. The audience began to dissolve.

"I think they hit him," Rogers said. "The nightfighters should get him before he gets too far away."

"The hell you say," Macon said. "They never touched him. What the hell, Buddy, wouldn't you dive and get all the speed up that you could if you were in that ship? Damn right you would, or they'd have plastered your butt against the north star. What do you think, Lloyd; did they hit him or not?"

"No, I don't think they did," Lloyd said.

"That'll be approximately 20 yen, please," Macon said. He lit up a cigarette, smiled smugly, plopped down on the edge of his cot and began to unlace his high-top combat shoes.

"I'll pay you tomorrow," Rogers said. "I'll have to borrow the money when I get back from the mission."

"Yeah," Macon said. "Well, don't go and auger in until you do pay up."

"Believe me," Rogers said, "that's the only reason that I want to get back—just to pay you."

"Yeah, I know," Macon said, "you'd rather owe it to me for life than cheat me out of it."

Lloyd was already in bed when Macon climbed into his netting, fought it into place and eased back on the pillow. Rogers finished undressing and stepped over to the center tent-pole, gave the light string a quick yank, dropped into bed. Rogers was the only one in the tent who wore any 'pajamas' and they consisted only of underwear shorts; nevertheless, Macon mused, he was almost always the last one to hit the sack. But, as he relaxed, Macon appreciated the man's tardiness, it meant that Rogers was left to turn out the light after Macon had enjoyed the aid of the light in adjusting his own comfort. The air raid had kept them up past their usual bedtime, it was nearly eleven o'clock now and the evening was getting cool—practically cool enough to sleep.

It wasn't yet four o'clock when the tent light went on again. Macon knew it wasn't four o'clock because the damp early morning chill had not as yet chased him inside his folded sheet. He hoisted himself to his left elbow, opened a sleep-filled eye, peered half-blindly at his watch. It was only one-fifteen.

Captain Goodman, bald, shirtless, with pants still unbuttoned and a half-spent cigar stuck in the left corner of his mouth, stood near the main tent-pole.

Lloyd was awake too. "What's the matter, Pop?" he said.

'Pop' Goodman was the Squadron Intelligence Officer and his nickname was one of endearment. It seemed that everyone liked Pop and no one ever spoke gruffly to him, for he would have taken it too much to heart. Pop, it was conceded, was a very sentimental soul.

He was surely an oddity, standing semi-nude in the middle of night, looking as though he had just rolled out of bed himself. He rubbed his bald spot, scratched the jet black fringe that perched above his left ear, rolled the cigar around in his mouth, made a directional jerk with his right thumb. Macon followed the direction of the manoeuvre and saw a young, dark, heavy-set lieutenant struggling through the door of the tent. He was weighted down with a bulging B-4 bag in one hand, a small stuffed overnight bag in the other, a musette bag over his shoulder.

"A new crew just arrived," Goodman said. "This

13

is the Navigator, Weaver."

"Hello," said Macon.

"Come in," said Bruce Lloyd cheerfully. "Make yourself to home, the word is welcome and the food is lousy." Lloyd, Macon mused, must be still half-asleep, for when in a half-conscious state he felt that his comic routine and clever patter came with effortless finesse. Macon fell back from his elbow to the pillow, rolled toward the activities and watched in unimpressed silence.

"Did you come up from Clark Field?" Lloyd asked. Macon realized that Lloyd was merely being polite and trying to make the newcomer feel at home. He lay quietly observing the charm.

"Yes," the newcomer said. "We came the long way, I guess. It took a hell of a long time to get here. We came in a C-46. Took us nearly six hours. They tried to fly formation with two other 46's. Didn't do a very good job."

How the hell would a Navigator know? Macon mused. If he didn't know that they were coming the long way, how the hell would he know they weren't flying good formation . . . ?

"Well, better get some sleep; besides, Rogers here has to fly tomorrow." Pop smiled and left with the air of a hotel manager who had just rented a new guest the best room in the place.

"Yeah," Lloyd said, "old Buck here has to get up at four-thirty."

"I'll turn the light off now then," Weaver said. He smiled as he did. "Buck Rogers; gee, that's a funny name."

Weaver was hauling the rest of his luggage into the darkened tent as Macon fell asleep.

14

CHAPTER II

A light rain was falling when Buck Rogers climbed out of bed in answer to the summons of the Operations Sergeant who came around to awaken the men on call. Buck was dressing in the darkness when Macon grumbled into consciousness.

"You awake, Make?" Rogers said.

"Guess?" Macon said. "What time is it?"

"Twenty to five. Sorry I woke you up." Rogers was a good-looking blond with curly hair and startling blue eyes. He was small, slight, with a happy air. It wasn't difficult to image why the twenty-year-old Flight Officer was so popular, even though he had been in the Squadron only about two and a half months. Why, everybody knew 'old' Buck, the kid with the beautiful wife. Everybody must have seen some of the many pictures that he proudly displayed; he had them in all conceivable shapes and sizes from wallet photos to life-size portraits. She was a small blonde, too, and it had taken Rogers some time to convince Macon that

15

she wasn't his sister.

"You're too young and she's too pretty," Macon had said. Buck would just smile, look at her picture, shake his head and dreamily agree that she was 'real pretty'.

Rogers was lacing up his shoes as Macon rolled over and blinked up at him through sleep-clouded eyes. "When's final briefing?"

"Six-forty. Wish I didn't have to go on this one."

"Shouldn't be too rough for you," Macon said. "And how those combat points add up."

"You know, Make," Rogers said, "I'm worried."

"Oh, please . . ." Macon said, with a low groan, "not so early in the morning."

"I don't *always* worry this early in the day."

"That should make your wife very happy."

"It's my wife that I'm worried about."

That subject—worrying about one's wife—always had a strange, sadistic fascination for Macon. He was at least 99 and 44/100 percent awake now. He folded his hands behind his head, looked up at the struggling Rogers who was fighting with the zipper on his coveralls. "What's she done?"

"Oh, it's not that!" Rogers said quickly. "Gee, what a mind you have!"

"I'll slap it," Macon said. "Remind me, will you?"

"That's what I'm worried about."

"What?" Macon scratched his head. "This is getting very confusing. Are you worried about me slapping my mind later, your wife—or just what the hell *is* bothering you, buddy?"

"Oh, I don't know . . ."

"Goddamn it," Macon said, sitting up. "You got me awake to tell me something, and now you'd better sound off . . ."

16

"Well," Rogers said, slowly. He was obviously thinking deeply about what he was going to say. He sat down on the chair in the center of the tent facing Macon's bed. "It's odd."

"I give up; what is?"

"Well, my mother sent me a letter; I got it about a month ago. She writes very often, you understand —it's just that I'm referring to this letter in particular. You understand?"

"Christ yes! Get on with the story . . ."

"Well, she told me that while my wife was visiting her, 'Chink,' my wife—her name's Cynthia— had an awful nightmare. She woke up screaming and crying; you know . . ." Rogers' story picked up speed as it went along; he seemed to be talking very fast. Macon noticed that Lloyd was awake, propped up on one elbow, listening. Rogers, by virtue of an occasional glance, acknowledged that he was including Lloyd in his audience. "Well, my wife never said anything about it; and I guess my mother didn't mean to, either. I guess it just slipped out. You know how things will in a letter. She didn't realize what she was saying. I just did get a sort of a hint; that was all. Well, I wrote and asked my wife what was the matter. You know, I even thought I might be having a baby—or, well, you know . . ." He looked at them to see if they did know. They seemed to understand, so he crossed his leg, went on, slower now, "You know, I didn't know what to think. I worried about her a lot. I love her." His eyes seemed to be 10,000 miles away. "But, she ignored the whole incident, and that made me insist all the harder. When it looked like we were on the verge of a fight, my mother figured it was time to settle it—she was right, too—we

17

probably would have had a fight; well, she told me about it—and now, finally, I can see why my wife wouldn't say . . ."

"What?" Lloyd said.

"She dreamt that I got killed . . ."

That one floored them—not even Macon could roll with it. It took him a long moment to recover. "Forget it," he said. "Forget it. Why, why I'd be dead a dozen times if what the girls I know dreamed about me came true."

Lloyd laughed, he was good on the uptake. "I'll bet you're right at that, Make," he said.

"Well, thanks," Macon said. "Thanks, I like you too."

Lloyd laughed. "You know, I believe you, Make." He laughed some more.

"Nuts," Macon said.

"Well, I've got to go, I guess," Rogers said. "But I certainly wish I didn't have to, today."

"Why today?" Macon said.

"I just feel superstitious, I guess," Rogers said. "You see, I got the letter from my mother—the one where she told me about what my wife dreamt—I got it yesterday."

"Forget it," Lloyd said. "Forget it, Buck. Everybody feels that way once in a while. Forget it."

Rogers adjusted his shoulder holster, patting it into place carefully. He checked his pockets to make sure that he had everything that he needed.

"Take it easy, Buck," Lloyd said. "I'll see you tonight."

Rogers grunted, went out. Macon dozed off. When he awoke the rain had stopped. It was seven-fifteen.

He yawned, blinked, rubbed his eyes, yawned

18

again, forced an opening in the side of the mosquito netting, swung his feet over the edge of the cot, sat up. "Let's go. Let's go," he announced. "Only fifteen minutes to get breakfast. Let's go." He sounded as though he was talking to himself, and as he spoke he began carefully to put on his shoes.

Lloyd stirred, showed definite signs of life. Weaver, the new man, was out of his netting quickly and began to dress. "You can't get breakfast after seven-thirty, is that right?" he said.

"Yeah," said Macon.

"I'm glad it stopped raining," Weaver said.

It sounded like a complete statement of a conclusive thought so no one answered him. He must have thus assumed that the early morning was not the time for socializing so he remained quiet. The other two men climbed silently into their clothes. Macon paused at a water-filled steel helmet resting upside down in a small ammunition box. He rinsed his hands, washed his face. Outside was a regular stand for the helmet that Lloyd used for a washbasin. The stand had four legs, built from the limbs of pine trees, with a shelf made from the side of a small ammunition box. The shelf ended halfway across the stand; the remainder of the space was occupied by the helmet itself. It was suspended among four smaller pieces of pine that formed a square frame. The back of the stand was built up to a height of nearly six feet with scraps of pine and discarded lumber; its purpose, to hold the mirror for the person performing his toilet, was thus gracefully accomplished. The beauty of the structure was of little concern. An Emergency Signaling Mirror (ESM/2), with a small cut-out cross in the center that was used for aiming, hung loosely from

19

the top of the stand and swung promiscuously in the occasional breezes that skipped across the valley.

When they had washed, Lloyd and Macon merely exchanged glances—the signal that they were prepared to leave—and started toward the Mess Hall. Weaver had had no water so he didn't wash and was ready early; now he fell in step behind them as they trudged off to breakfast.

The Mess Hall was, in reality, merely a kitchen; the kitchen was, in reality, merely a tent. The stoves, the pots and pans and bread boxes and olive drab number-ten cans of food were all jammed into this cramped space in an ordinary square four-man tent. Outside, on the north side of the tent, was a serving line. This structure consisted of two orange crates with a long 2"x8" plank across the tops. On the board were set the tubs and jars that contained the meal. The men filed quickly past the service counter with their mess kits outstretched, the handles of their canteen cups stuck outside their belts so as to provide one free hand for the manipulation of the food.

Macon and his companions got their food, hunted for a place to settle down to eat it. There were no tables or chairs or even noticeably level ground. The Group having just moved into Okinawa from Leyte would be forced to function in the temporary set-up until the arrival of the 'water echelon' that was en route on an LST. The men nearby were sitting on old boxes, spent number-ten cans (which left something to spare and much to be desired), rocks, flat pieces of cardboard, or the ground itself. Some were standing beside the various vehicles in the area, using a fender or the top of a motor for a table. There were no such vacancies at the moment, however, since these final fifteen minutes before the mess closed were always the busiest. Macon led the trio to a small knoll where they sat on the wet ground, finished their pancakes and coffee without speaking.

At seven-twenty-five sharp the Group took off. When they left the runway heading north, as they did that day, the men looked up from their meals, quietly, reverently watched. Every ten seconds a plane would roar over the hill that separated the strip from the mess hall area, vibrate past within a half mile of these spectators, then thunder away as only a B-25 could. When the two dozen aircraft had been egged, observed and tabulated successfully the men washed their mess kits, left.

The rain had been falling periodically since the Group moved onto the island and the ground was soft. However, for the past week there had been only light, quick showers and the walking wasn't impossible. When they returned to their tent, Macon took his helmet and went around to the back, the south side of the tent, to pick some of the rainwater that had collected on the canvas. He held out his helmet, reached in under the flap and tapped the underside of the roof gently, causing the water to jump and drain slowly into the waiting receptacle. Weaver watched Macon with some admiration and carefully studied Lloyd's performance in repeating the process. The busy pair then proceeded to wash and shave.

Weaver stood in the center of the tent and allowed his eyes to digest his new surroundings. Macon could feel the newcomer's devouring glance as definitely as he could feel his razor scrape the cold

21

water lather from his chin. Weaver said nothing as he appraised the place like a young bride moving into her first home. The flaps on the front of the tent were rolled, the top canvas doors tied together so that entrance could be gained only by bending and ducking under the section of the roof. The two sides and the rear were elongated, the flaps having been unrolled and stretched horizontally across the tops of upright four-and-a-half foot tent-poles and each pole anchored with a tent rope and stake; six of these staffs and outriggers, three on either side of the door, held the front in place. The four cots ran front or rear in the tent, Macon's being in the rear left (looking out the front door), Lloyd's in the rear right, Rogers' front left, Weaver's front right. The cots were foot-to-foot.

Near the head of Lloyd's cot three 14" x 8" x 6" dynamite boxes were built into a makeshift bookcase. It was mounted on a larger orange crate and rested on the top of a small mound of dirt that had been carefully constructed for the purpose. In front of the dynamite shelves, beside his cot, Lloyd had nailed three 1" x 8" planks together as a piece of flooring, for the tent's floor was of dirt. Beside the shelves was a heavy pine limb stuck upright with a small lumber crossbar which held five tenpenny box nails and from which suspended Lloyd's B-4 bag, raincoat, flying coveralls, two T-shirts, a towel.

Near Macon's bed stood a cabinet affair composed of two orange boxes placed one atop the other. There was also a clothes stand similar to Lloyd's and four scraps of lumber of varying sizes resting casually on the dirt floor, looking more like a rock garden than a bit of flooring. Rogers' corner was comparatively simple. Next to the foot of his cot an orange crate resting on its side held a pair of shoes, a few beer cans and two miscellaneously-filled cigar boxes on the bottom level; toilet articles, three assorted bottles scented with personal privacy, a photo of his wife, and two packs of cigarettes on the top. Near the crate a straight-back bamboo chair, conceived by some friendly natives on Leyte, overflowed with clothing and flying equipment. A B-4 bag and a parachute A-3 bag were thrust under the bed. The other chair, a folding, cloth-gutted beach chair, stood close to the main tent-pole. Weaver began to unpack his baggage.

Lloyd moved out onto the soft dirt before the tent, into the morning sun that was struggling with some large, fluffy cumulus clouds to keep its place in the broken sky. He dropped down on one of the two empty dynamite boxes that were the "front porch." He was working over a pair of low-cut civilian shoes when Macon brought out the beach chair, sat beside him and watched inquisitively.

"I'm trying to get some of this damn mold off these shoes," Lloyd said.

"Okay," Macon said simply.

"Well," Lloyd said, "I wanted to get your permission." He smiled.

Macon lit a cigarette, gazed disinterestedly about the squadron area. The tent was in the first of the three rows of officers' tents and the ground fell away before his chair to the dirt road that bounded through the area and linked them with the rest of the world. Across the street the Orderly Tent, Operations Tent, Intelligence Tent, Supply Tent, Communications Tent, Gunnery Tent were beginning to show signs of activity. Behind this row, still further north, the enlisted men's tents were getting their flaps rolled, their beds made. West of the EM area the mess tent was cleaning its pots and putting out its garbage. A weapons-carrier truck towed a water trailer up the company street, slid around the corner and up the little mud drive to the mess tent, oozed to a slithering stop in front of the serving line, unburdened itself. Before the truck had had time to execute its slippery exit thirsty tubs and impatient pitchers were suckling the trailer, prompted by busy cooks and kaypees.

The supply jeep, two operations jeeps, and a gunnery-weapons carrier were parked, nose in, just off the other side of the road. A big six-by-six truck growled past in second gear carrying a dozen men to a distant detail. Captain Brown, Squadron operations chief, came out of the tent next door, waved left-handed greetings toward Macon and Lloyd, trotted down the small incline, went across the street into his office.

Lloyd was still scraping the mold from his first shoe with his long trench knife when Weaver came out to watch.

"How quickly do things get moldy here?" he said, as he sat down on the other unoccupied box.

"Oh, don't worry about it for a while," Macon said, "not for a week or so anyway."

"I don't think the leather is moldy," Lloyd said, ignorning Macon, "it's the saddle soap I put on a couple of weeks ago at Leyte. There I figured I needed some saddle soap to preserve them; here I think the saddle soap itself gets moldy."

"This joker's always saddle-soaping his shoes or cleaning his .45 or washing socks or fixing his truss or some damn thing or other," Macon said. "He always fluffs around here like a butler, or a handyman or house detective, or something equally suspicious. He beats the hell out of my sacktime, because I'm always afraid I'll miss something. He keeps me awake hour after hour, for two and three hours on end sometimes."

Weaver smiled politely, waited for Macon to reflect for a moment in the light of his sparkling comedy, spoke again. "Do you think shirts or other clothing will get moldy here? One of my shirts got moldy on the way over."

Lloyd shook his head. "I doubt it. Not if you keep your stuff dry." He went on with his scraping. "And if you see any signs of decay, hang your stuff out in the sun for a day or two; that should fix it up okay."

"Only trouble with that sunshine theory," Macon said, "is that the sun rains damn wet around here."

"You got in kind of late last night," Lloyd said, ignoring Macon with such ease that one could intimate that he had had much practice ignoring Macon. "Did Pop get a chance to orientate you?"

"Oh, you mean Captain Goodman?" Weaver said. "No, he didn't. We got in late and he only had time to give us our mailing address."

"Well, don't fret," Macon said, "he'll nail you quick. He'll tell you all about the Group and the Squadron and tell you what you can write and can't write and fill you with enough patriotism that even your shortest letter home will send the home-folks sprinting out to buy more war bonds."

"Nuts," Lloyd said. "Pop does a damn fine job."

"Granted. But Pop doesn't give us all the fruit of the bruit."

"If you want rumors, go to the latrine," Lloyd snorted.

"Well," Macon said, "I've been constipated and haven't heard anything spicy for nearly a week, since I can't see going there just for the trip."

"As I was saying, before Macon dragged himself into the latrine," Lloyd said, "if there are any questions you want to ask about the outfit, Weaver, I'll try to help as best I can."

"Thanks, I do have some."

"He was here when it was really rough," Macon laughed. "So if you have a problem . . ."

"Fire away." Lloyd turned away from Macon, who was on his right. "You can't take this character too seriously, you know," Lloyd told Weaver, "or he'll start you wondering why the hell we're winning this war. All the pilots in the Squadron aren't this bad. Some of them like old Buck, or Brownie, are even reasonably sane."

"If I had a beautiful woman like Buck's got," Macon said, "I'd be sane too; I think, I think, I think." He made a couple of playful epileptic twitches with his chin and arm.

"Ignore him, he might go away," Lloyd said.

"I was just wondering what kind of missions the Group flies," Weaver explained. "I know it's a strafer outfit, but in B-25 R.T.U. training in Greenville we didn't do much low-flying."

"The South Carolina Chapter of the Fraternity is definitely against buzzing," Macon said. "But you'll get all you can handle over here."

"And then some," Lloyd said. "If you come over the target above ten or fifteen feet you're too damn high."

"And you will probably get your butt shot full of

bird-shot," Macon said. "If you ever heard about the cadet who was told by his mother to fly low and slow, forget it; here you firewall everything. You get more speed out of these gas buggies than even North American thought possible. And, buddy, you really hug the ground. You use every tree and hill for cover."

"Every tree?"

"Roger. And the big bushes too, if you can find them," Macon said. "Those Jap pom-pom batteries are rough, they'll hang your jock for you in a flash, if you give them a chance. Those jokers can shoot!"

"How do you make your pass?" Weaver said.

"On a big freighter, a 'sugar able sugar' for instance, or a destroyer you go in three abreast," Macon said. "On smaller ones, two abreast or alone. Land targets are different; you only go over them once—twenty-four abreast."

"You go over shipping more than once." Weaver wasn't asking, he seemed rather to be turning the thought over in his mind.

"You go over them until they sink, or you're out of bombs and ammo." Macon sat back in the easy chair, lit a cigarette. "And if you think that you'll be low on land targets, wait until you go after shipping!"

"Why, what do you mean?"

"You get low enough to strike up a conversation with the fish and when you line up for a pass you get your interval—about fifty or a hundred feet— and you don't vary it. All your evasive action is up and down, up and down, and the lower you get the harder it is for those jokers to shoot at you because their guns won't go very much below zero elevation."

"How high are you when you drop your bombs?"

"You pull up to about fifty feet," Lloyd said.

"But I'm just wasting my time here," Macon said, suddenly. "What good does it do to talk shop with two navigators? What good are navigators?"

Lloyd cut in again. "How about Formosa," he said in a flat matter-of-fact voice.

"We don't talk about that."

"He was lost bigger than hell up there," Lloyd explained. "He got separated from the formation and the navigator was hit and he had to find his own way home. He took the long way around, too; and after some fancy navigation on his part he landed, with sixteen gallons of gas left. He made the tightest pattern I've ever seen when he came in on his approach. He came in at 300 feet, yelling hysterically over the VHF, dropped wheels and flaps and set it down without even getting permission from the tower."

"I had a wounded man aboard," Macon said.

"Well, why did you take so long in coming home?" Lloyd chided. "Were you on the forty-cent tour?" Lloyd laughed. "The guys have never stopped razzing him about the whole eyedropper of gas he brought back, and wasted."

"Trouble with this joker is that he can't take a joke," Macon said.

"Every guy who's ever had to fly with this cross between a peasant and a trapper has had to take a joke," Lloyd said, pressing the attack good-naturedly.

"Do you mean they break the crew up here?" Weaver asked.

"Yeah," Lloyd said. "Strafer outfits usually do."

"Who decides who flies with what crew?"

"Brownie, the operations chief," Lloyd said. "He posts the list at about six o'clock in the evening and

28

Group briefing is usually before the movie, at about six-thirty. Squadron briefing is in the morning after breakfast."

"In other words, it's just pot luck?"

"That's about it," Macon said. "You see, the first pilots go out as co-pilots for eight or ten missions to learn our procedure and then they move over to the left seat. That means that he's late and his co-pilot is even later in getting started; meanwhile the rest of the crew is flying regularly. However, if a pilot is in solid with operations chief, or he sounds off loud enough and long enough he can usually get to fly with the crew he brought overseas with him. But by that time it isn't worth the bother for the couple of missions that the crew would be together. This way everybody flies with everybody else; it's quite sociable."

"And if it's that pilot's turn to hang his jock, you get it too," Weaver said flatly.

"Roger. Isn't that always the way?" Macon flicked his cigarette out into the street, some thirty feet away. "If you're going to auger in, you auger in and worrying about it won't keep you the slightest bit drier."

"Oh, I'm a fatalist, too," Weaver said. "What is to be, is to be, and all that."

"That's about the size of it," Macon said. "I've seen some awfully good pilots in this Squadron crack up. At ten feet, going over 300 miles per hour it requires a very small mistake to do the job. Errors, real sloppy ones, made at 6,000 or 8,000 feet don't mean a thing except that you have to recover; but a slip down 'on the deck' means that you've got hardships."

"We do lose a big percent of our casualties

29

through operational losses," Lloyd said. "It's listed as pilot error, I suppose, but, hell, nobody's perfect —and when you've got only one mistake to use up: well, you'd just better not make them, that's all."

"The Japs have a few real cute tricks on land targets," Macon said. "They string wires between the tops of the taller trees in the vicinity and if you hit the wires it's just tough cigar. At Balikpapan they had very high trees and they got quite a few jokers with their wires. Oh, another dilly is when they put charges of dynamite on the tops of the trees. You usually bring home a few leaves and branches anyway since you're always right down in the trees on your target run and if you hit a charge of TNT, then school is really out."

"Oh," Weaver said.

"Oh, don't get me wrong," Macon said quickly, "it's not bad, really. That's just the worst of it. You really do have fine fun strafing everybody and everything."

"Civilians too?"

"What are they?" Macon said. "I don't ever recall hearing the term. Have you Lloydie?"

"No; can't say that I ever have. Everybody works in a home industry in Japan, that removes them from the civilian class."

"You mean you strafe cities?" Weaver asked.

"Cities, towns, villages, boats, civilians, outhouses, everything," Macon smiled. "We eliminate the negative; that's our specialty and our charm. Tokyo Rose has offered a reward of ten thousand American dollars for any member of the 'Butchering 999th Group,' taken alive, of course. That's a lot of yen, you know."

"In other words," Lloyd added, "don't get forced

down in Japan. There is no way that I know of avoiding it; but, just don't."

"I was going to ask if you carried your .45's on missions," Weaver said. "I heard that they weren't carrying them in the ETO."

"You'll carry them here," Macon said, "and you'll carry a couple of extra clips and all the hardware you can find."

"You'll go out of here looking like Captain Blood himself," Lloyd said. "And, if you wear that flak suit you'll look like a man from Mars or a fugitive from last season's Sears and Roebuck catalogue."

"Does everybody wear a flak suit?" Weaver asked.

"No," Lloyd said, "but nobody will laugh at you if you do."

Weaver offered his cigarettes around; Macon accepted one and waited for Weaver to light him. They sat in silence and smoked. The traffic began to breathe heavier now, it was getting on toward nine o'clock.

"Well," Macon said, as he stood up and stretched, "this mad pace is making a nervous wreck of me." He flipped his cigarette, turned and went into the tent.

"Where's he going?" Weaver asked.

Lloyd flipped his cigarette. "To hit the sack." He took up his trench knife and again began to scrape the mold off of his shoes.

CHAPTER III

It was eleven-fifteen when Macon awoke. The other two men were in bed also. Weaver was asleep, but Lloyd was conscious, laying on his back looking up at the roof. It hadn't taken the newcomer long to become indoctrinated, Macon mused. Just learn to relax and await your turn, just lay and wait and wait and wait. Macon swung his legs over the side of the cot, sat up.

Bruce Lloyd's eyes followed him, although the head didn't move. "Is it that time?"

"Yeah, let's go." Macon put his boots on, arose without lacing them. "Look at America's fighting man there," he said, nodding toward the sleeping Weaver.

Lloyd struggled into his heavy G.I. shoes and followed Macon out, nudging Weaver as he went. Weaver came to with a start, popped out of bed, plunged into his brogans, came lumbering along behind them.

They walked down the incline to the street, crossed over to the Intelligence Tent. Macon went in followed by Lloyd and Weaver, who had caught up with them. Pop Goodman sat at a crude table writing a letter. The tent looked cold, bare, even in the intense noonday heat. The table, with a cellophane-covered map of the immediate theatre of operations serving as a top, posed awkwardly in the nearby corner. A larger table, a low longish bench, and a half-dozen assorted empty boxes constituted the remaining furniture. On the canvas wall that partitioned the Intelligence Office from the quarters of the office personnel a large, used map and a well-populated rectangular bulletin board held the detailed information about the day's mission.

"Hi, men," Pop said. "Hello, Weaver; did you get settled okay? Make here let you stay, didn't he?" He laughed, put aside his pen. "You'll find after a little while that his bark is worse than his bite."

"Oh, yes indeed, Captain," Weaver said. "Everything's just fine."

"Auger Inn treats guests, friends and in-laws with the same jim-dandy hospitality that has made it the most famous hole since Calcutta," Macon said.

"I remember once . . ." Pop said.

"Hold on, hold on," Macon said, "everybody's making up filthy stories about me. Don't you believe any of them, Weaver. You alone know how sweet and innocent I am."

"As I was saying," Pop laughed, "I remember one time at Leyte at the club bar when you threw out that guy from the 659th. Boy, what a . . ."

"Well," Macon said, "let's go to chow."

"Okay, I'll write my letter." Goodman picked up his pen and started to write again.

"You come in here when you want to see the

strike pictures of the mission flown the previous day," Lloyd was explaining to Weaver. They had walked across the sawdust covered dirt floor and were studying the pictures on the bulletin board. There were nine photos of a small town that the Group had hit. "The cameras are mounted aft of the radio compartment," Lloyd said.

"Any strike report, Pop?" Macon said.

"Nothing yet, Make."

"Do you think they'll find that shipping?" Macon said.

"It was all up near the Shimonoseki Straights, according to the Snooper reports last night, so if we don't hear within about a half hour it will mean that they had to go to the secondary."

Lloyd and Weaver were studying the pictures, Bruce speaking softly and pointing out and explaining the targets to the new man. Macon offered a cigarette to Pop, who declined and took out a cigar instead. Pop lit them both with his battered black Zippo lighter.

"Got a letter from my wife," Pop said. "She says the youngest one is beginning to talk now."

"Oh, so?" Macon said, half-watching the two men at the board.

"Says two or three words at a time," Pop said. "Even speaks whole sentences sometimes."

"Can't understand it," Macon said. "The old man isn't clever at all. The mother must be smart."

"Well, I won't argue that point," Pop laughed.

"Come on, you guys," Macon said, impatiently moving toward the door of the tent. "Let's go."

A sergeant came down the makeshift dirt sidewalk that ran beside the street in front of the row of office tents.

"Here comes the strike report now," Pop said, watching the man approach the tent. "They must have hit shipping."

The sergeant came bursting in. He looked excited and spoke quickly to Goodman as he entered. "One of ours is down, Captain! The report just came through."

"You sure it's from this Squadron?" Goodman said.

"The Group lead element is the 659th and their report to Group Operations said one of ours. Didn't say who though."

Macon walked out of the tent; Weaver and Lloyd followed. They left Pop sadly scratching the small amount of jet-black hair that was still his and trudged to the mess hall to the sound of the rattle of their mess gear.

Halfway through the bully beef and canned tomatoes Lloyd put down his fork. "I wonder who it was."

Macon shrugged. He was munching thoughtfully on a piece of bread and jam. There was no butter. "Goddamn it, I wish they'd get some butter around here," he said.

They finished their canned peaches, waited in line at the large G.I. cans to scrub out their mess kits, then walked silently back to the tent. Macon crossed over to his cot, flopped down on it; Weaver began puttering about in his B-4 bag; Lloyd stood in the center of the floor idly eyeing Rogers' bed.

"Let's play some pinochle," Macon said suddenly. "It's too early to mourn him; he may surprise us and turn up."

"Okay," Lloyd said. "Do you play, Weaver?" He

35

received an affirmative nod. "We can play on my bed; I'll get a box from outside." He got the seat and took some cards from his top shelf, shuffled and dealt.

Weaver, straddling the head of the cot, opened with a bid of twenty. Macon, knees crossed, at the foot of the bed, said twenty-one. Lloyd said twenty-two. Weaver said twenty-three. Macon passed, let his glance slide easily from the game, through the open sides of the tent to the noonday traffic on the street, to the neighbors sleeping off their dinner in their open canvas houses, to a couple of the Squadron's pets playing in dog-like fashion to Captain Brown climbing into his jeep and leading a cloud of dust out of the area. Macon digested the tranquility of this peaceful island that held so much power of war. Only the roar of an occasional airplane broke the magic spell of this oasis of peace. Y-shaped Okinawa, the largest member of the Ryukyu Island chain, eased its bumpy, pockmarked face into azure water that looked from the air like a continuation of the blue sky. The chain of islands stood like bumps on the ocean between Okinawa and Kyushu, landmarks running exactly parallel and a dozen miles east of the shortest route between these two points. The Ryukyus, oval Yaku Jima, oblong Tanegashima and all the other occasional tiny islands that thrust their coral and rock straight up and out of the water punctuated the 325 nautical miles to Markurazaki on the southern tip of Japan, like granite hermits.

Okinawa itself had surprised Macon when he first saw it. For the first time in the Pacific he saw grass and pine trees that had a nodding acquaintance with the scenery back home. Hills, literally hundreds of them; small, abrupt, severe, jutting from the ground as a mixture of coral and grass and disappearing into tangled underbrush and then nothing, like welts in all stages of formation and dissipation. They appeared warped, squashed, like mounds with contours of every possible distortion— with wide valleys and valleys that were long and short and narrow and deep and shallow between every pair of uprisings. It was a land of irregular dimples knotted together with a series of loops that would drive a deck-sailor to drink. There was grass in abundance, too; and rich brown dirt, and weeds and tangled shrubbery that had been nourished on neglect, but which, nevertheless, looked like American species of weeds and undergrowth. But, of course, there was the ever-present Pacific Ocean coral—jagged and sharp and blinding in the sunlight. Rocks of coral abandoned homes with walls of coral brick, coral protruding from the roads and the fields, coral forming a broken floor for the beach, it was as ever-present as the war.

Now, as Okinawa's July of 1945 was spending itself dispatching air raids, moving the freight of the hundreds of offshore boats into depots for disposal, and warming up for August, the Navy Seabees were blasting away mountains of coral and pounding them into runways long enough to receive General Doolittle's B-29's.

The Seabees, however, were dealing but a small portion of the bustle and tumult—which is to guarantee the fervor of the activity to anyone who has ever seen the swarming Seabees make mountains into miracles; roads were conceived and nurtured, stretched and twisted, coraled and bulldozed until

37

they covered the island like a face net. Runways and taxi-ways hatched mysteriously, tents had appeared without warning among the trees and beside the natives' tombs, making Okinawa look from the air like a crawling ant hill. These tombs, symbols of oriental devotion to the dead, were massive open-faced battleship-grey coral and coral cement structures with small porch-like constructions in front. Entrance into the tomb itself was gained through a small door in the thick rampart and disclosed the bodies of the native ancestors. Immediately after its demise, the corpse is placed in a wooden coffin on the floor of the tomb, in the same doubled position as an unborn babe in the womb. The theory subscribed to is that during the period following death the spirit is reborn into a new world. Food and water is left in the tomb with the body for the journey, and the tomb is sealed. Three years after, a virgin is sent into the vault to take the bones from the original plain wooden casket and place them in an earthen urn. Thus the ancestors remained within easy range and the natives could go to report the occurrence of anything vital to them.

These tombs overtaxed the island's ability to digest them; they stood side by side in series of three's and four's or alone. Each new hill brought with it the view of more native tombs. Everywhere on this island, where the irregularity of landscape and beach was the most constant feature, these huge coral tombs looked like robust monsters lying stretched out on their backs on the sides of the land. This deathlike serenity punctuated the solemnity of the scene for each tomb itself, or its horseshoe-shaped protective coral wall that ran up the side of its hill, over the top of the crypt and down had been chipped or holed by gunfire of the intense battle that had raged here only a month or so before.

Lloyd won the first game of pinochle and dealt to begin the second. Macon's hands persisted; he lit a cigarette while waiting for the other two men to decide who would buy the bid. Weaver took it, named spades trump. Enthusiasm came to Macon in a rush for practically the first time; he had five trump.

"Katie, bar the door," he said, as he happily trumped the first trick. "Katie, bar the door!"

"This distribution makes you the big wheel in this game, doesn't it?" Lloyd said.

"Buddy, I'm really wheelin' and dealin' them this trip," Macon said. He laughed and flipped his cigarette out through the open side of the tent. "Wheelin' and dealin', wheelin' and dealin'. Leave me see now, how I can screw up the detail for you, Weaver, my boy. . . ."

They set Weaver, and Macon was mischievously delighted; he settled back, lit up another cigarette. Above the taunts of his riotous gaiety, the blaring engines of B-25's suddenly and subtly became audible. Weaver, the dealer, placed the cards on the bed and helped the others listen. Lloyd nervously chewed at a fingernail. Macon rolled his cigarette between his fingers, watching the smoke dreamily rise.

Macon got up and followed Lloyd outside. The other tents in the area were emptying quiet, sky-gazing men. No one spoke loudly; everyone studied the direction that was now giving full vent to the roaring Wright engines. The hill to the north still

39

concealed the identity of the lost crew to them. The men stood about in various stages of undress, hands on hips or in pockets, smoking, watching, waiting for the Mitchell formation that had left that morning as a twenty-four-ship task force bring its twenty-three survivors in over the area in the daily gesture of arrival.

Macon lit a new cigarette from the glow of the spent one, threw the used one away. This sort of thing made him nervous; this waiting to discover the truth was the real strain of war. But now, the answer would soon be known. The squadron formation would have a gaping cavity and everyone would know by the position of the remaining five planes. The sweating out of this mission was nearly over. The engines sounded louder, the pilots would be jockeying into a tight formation—five or ten feet between planes, close on the leader; it had to be tight, it had to look good when you came back from a mission. You had to look your best and circle the field and peel off sharply as P-40's, in five-second intervals, then race around the short pattern, drop your flaps and wheels and come in. But it had to look good and the formation had to be close; even though the mountains' updrafts and downdrafts bounced your ship about like a wayward jeep—close in and look good, you had to keep it tight; the parade had to look proud!

The 659th Squadron, Lobster One for the strike, eased over the mountain heading south to the strip toward the straining eyes of the men of the 606th who were sweating out their buddies. The first flight, three planes in the V-formation employed by each element of the various Squadrons, led the 659th across the crest of the hill. The 990th Squadron,

Lobster Two (each Squadron in the Group was designated Lobster One, Two, Three or Four, depending on each day's flight orders and thus the Group lead rotated) came over on the 659th right wing. Lobster Three, the 989th Squadron, was on the leader's left wing.

Lobster Four alone was still out of sight. Now the first element came over: Big Captain Michelson, Squadron commander, was leading. Flipowitz was in number two on his right; Bonelli came up on the left tucked in close. The first flight was all present.

Rogers had been flying in number five when they went out, with O'Toole leading the second element in number four position, and Sammy Meade occupying number six. It had to be one of these three!

Two planes moved across the ridge. The element had a leader and a left wingman! It was either O'Toole, with Rogers moved up to take over, or it was Rogers. The men hurried across the street to the Operations Tent. Brownie had the Tower on the phone. They were checking the numbers of the planes in the pattern; he was getting the answer for them.

He spoke a few, quick words into the mouthpiece, the silence was so heavy that his conversation was undiscernible to Macon. Brown hung up, sighed. "Number 879 is back. That's O'Toole's ship. Rogers is missing."

They had their answer. Macon walked slowly across the street, stepped up the small incline, sat down in the beach chair, lit a cigarette. It was hard to comprehend that Buck was gone. Buck, who had walked out of the tent about eight hours before as though he were stepping out for a cup of coffee,

41

would never return. The airman's war, they said, was impersonal and clean. Macon guessed maybe it was. You never saw your friends die, you never heard a hurt groan from any of them; they just walked out one day and they never came back. Rogers was clean-shaven and fairly well-fed when he went screaming in on that boat; probably the Jap seamen were wearing clean clothes too— But the water came up fast for he was hurtling along at over 300 miles per hour, and when he hit he was just as dead as he would have been had he been hit flush in the face by a German .88. Rogers hadn't had time to be thoroughly scared. It was a clean kill, no time for excitement, no time for prayers, just a fleeting fraction of a moment and it was over. Macon had seen it before. He had seen two B-25's crash on missions. When they hit the water they bounced, they exploded in a cloud of flying water and debris; they rolled sometimes, too, but nearly always they bounced and nearly always they came apart like somebody getting air-sick. They nearly always exploded in a quick, violent eruption that filled the air with water and perhaps a wheel or a piece of wing that you could see; or an arm or a tooth that whizzed past too fast for the eye to follow. They were right beside you one minute and then they hit so closely that you felt as though you could reach down and grab the plane by the nape of the neck and pull it out of danger. But, they hit, and they exploded quickly and the deed was done, and thirty seconds later the curious sharks might find a navigator's log or a piece of a Mae West lifejacket floating serenely at the site. But seldom more. In a flash the plane, its six men, the things in life that they felt needed their care were done;

done and gone and finished as thoroughly as violent death and countless fathoms of water could satisfy their lust. Perhaps death that came that quickly and that clean-shavenly compensated for dying; Macon doubted it. Death was all, and when the broken body lay beneath the vast volume of the endless, shark-filled Pacific it was death that was the end in every essence of finality; it was an airplane and six men who all crumpled like accordions and came apart. Macon respected death, because in its stubborn way it always had the last say.

The crowd before the Operation Tent had nearly dissipated and the area grew still as the men started to swarm about the mess tent. Tomorrow's mission would be speculated over the evening meal, then the list of those to fly it would be posted by Captain Brown and Group Briefing would earn for those present the army's last official funeral mention for the deceased—it would be a statement on the cause of the loss. The army would want to know why it had lost that airplane and its investment of six trained personnel; it was as cold-blooded as that, as cut-and-dried as rigid figures—figures to be deleted, items to be subtracted from the First Sergeant's morning report and the Engineer's record. Then the Supply Sergeant would send the personal effects home, and the incident would be closed.

Lloyd and Weaver sat beside Macon now. They were both smoking so Macon lit up another cigarette.

"You don't have an air mattress," Macon said to Weaver. "Might as well take Buck's."

Weaver said nothing. He looked as though he

43

wanted someone else to speak.

"I'm going to take his fountain pen and this chair," Macon said. "I broke my pen last month."

"Do you mean you take his stuff and he's only been dead a couple of hours?" Weaver asked. He looked as though he was shocked.

"If we don't get it that soon, we won't get it at all," Macon said. "A thousand jokers will be over soon and they'll pick his stuff over. They'll pick it clean, too; so, if you want anything you had better take it now."

"But don't they send that stuff home?" Weaver demanded.

"What good would it do them to get it?" Lloyd said. "It's no good to them and we can use it. They usually get one uniform complete with all the brass."

"But the personal stuff?" Weaver said.

"If you can convince the guys that his family can find some better use for his clean clothes than we can, they probably woud send all of his 150 pounds of luggage home," Macon said. "Complete with dirty socks, Pilot's Information File and toothpaste. But he's gone. That's that. They won't be his clothes tomorrow, they'll belong to somebody else."

"How about pictures and letters, and stuff like that," Lloyd said. "What about that stuff?"

"And fountain pens?" Macon said. "That's what you mean, isn't it? That stuff should be sent home, I suppose. But I need a pen, so I'll keep it." He studied his cigarette for a moment, then flicked it out into the street. "Weaver, you ask too many questions." He stood up. "Let's go to chow."

CHAPTER IV

Rain came to Okinawa during the third week of July with a vengeance. The steady, daily downpours turned the island into a half-sunken quagmire that made walking a risky task and caused what little activity there was to be reduced to a snail's wiggle. Rain that drove straight down or blew through the sides of the tent had turned the top layer of soil into an inert mass of chocolate brown goo that simmered and made a crackly, suction-like noise, like a water plunger, when someone tried to walk in it. The mud on Okinawa was heavy, it was as cumbersome as an unconscious drunk, and it was everywhere. It was in the roads, in the mess halls, in the offices, in the tents, in the men's shoes, in their clothes and their hair, in their beds. It spread like a plague, it clung like a bad relative or a nightmare, and it became as familiar to the men as their hands. It changed constantly, varied under each pedal impression that oozed out new pock-marks in its face, it was cruel and ever-ready to slip the feet out from under the unsuspecting. The mud tried every trick it knew to make the men miserable, and usually was quite successful.

Beneath the top layer nature had placed, if not a bonafide booby trap, then certainly a definite hazard. Under the impotent gooey surface a somewhat harder and very slippery bed of mire combined with the loose muck to form a clayish substance that was slippery as wet snow. Each new day found the same people slipping, sliding and crashing into the mud in their futile attempts to ease themselves down the incline to the area street. By July twenty-fourth, Captain Brown had taken to running down and Pop Goodman was toying with the idea of moving his cot over into the Intelligence Tent. At least the weather was able to furnish food for conversation, for talk was a difficult dish on Okinawa.

The rain fascinated Macon. As he watched the downpour from the comfort of his cot, he told himself that this rain had no character. In the States, weather built itself into a powerful, blowing force, before releasing its deluge. Here it merely seemed as though someone had turned on the showers and the rain just spilled. It definitely had no character. It was stupid, too. Very often rain teemed on Okinawa in the face of bright sunshine; it seemed as though the water wasn't aware of the fact that it and the sun could not occupy the scene together. The weather was too dumb to come in out of the sun. It was stupid and quite stubborn. It was stubborn inasmuch as a perfectly clear starlit night would ease aside ever so slightly to allow passage to a small, insignificant white cloud and the result would invariably be a ten or fifteen-minute downpour. It was stubborn, too, in that it poured with a vengeance quite often. Beneath the leaks in his tent, the wet night would find an innocent soldier struggling to get his cot and mosquito netting to a place of arid safety and the unrelenting weather would not only grow more severe but would unquestionably instigate another leak or two, thus chasing him about the tent with the tenacity of a lascivious bull.

The man-made counter-attack began during the first week that Group spent on the island. A half-dozen truckloads of crushed coral from the Engineer's pit became a sidewalk in front of the official tents across the street and floors for the tents themselves. However, no aid did seem forthcoming for the waterlogged dinette. The vicinity of the mess kitchen resembled the aftermath of the Johnstown flood, and since there was no room inside the tent for the serving counter, the food was usually flavored with water splashes or diluted by rain. The seating accommodations fared even worse. Pieces of cardboard boxes that had served as pads only a few hours before, weren't fit for anything better than a place to step. The number-ten cans that were pressed into service as dehydrated seats, and orange crates as the junior-sized tables were all laboring under chunks of mud and a vast percent of the previous day's garbage. To Macon the whole business had become a stinking mess!

The inclement weather had brought Macon's war to a standstill. Everything was grounded; even the birds seemed to be walking. For nearly a week he had been held firmly in the throes of horizontal boredom, for he was long since convinced that the average combat flier weekly (and weakly) logged many, many more hours in the sack than in the wild blue. Especially now, when the wild blue was a drab, sagging, tattletale grey. The only operations on the island were the periodic blasts set by the mountain-busting Seabees, and the animated rumors that insisted the B-29's had been scheduled to begin flying missions from neighboring Bolo Strip on August fifteenth. The deep-throated explosions, with their vibrating echoes bouncing finally into shaky silence, always came as a startling surprise. The louder ones would actually wake a man up. Even so, Macon managed to slumber through the majority.

By the twenty-fourth of July, even Macon felt bedridden and impatient with the inactivity. He tried to read, couldn't get interested, so he abandoned it.

Lloyd put aside the novel he was reading, struggled to an elbow, idly watched Macon begin a game of solitaire.

Macon returned his look. "Well, Zip; what can I do for you?"

"Nothing. Nothing at all," Lloyd said. "I just figured you must be getting bedsores; you've been horizontal for a week."

"Take a break, kid; I didn't hear anyone ask you."

"Sue me," Lloyd said, and returned to his book.

Macon finished his card game, thoroughly dissatisfied, and threw down the cards. "Where's Weaver?"

"He's not bothering you; leave him alone."

"I was just wondering. There's no reason for you to blow your top."

"Well, you just finished a long term on the pad and then blew your stack at me. What the hell do

48

you expect?" Lloyd turned ove on his side. "Excuse me; the ungarbled word now is that I want to go back to my story."

Macon sat in the beach chair in the center of the tent and smoked a cigarette. Weaver came in.

"No flights again tomorrow," he said. "The whole island is inoperative. Everything's grounded."

"Don't be so eager, birdman," Macon said. "You'll get your chance to win the war."

"It's the first one that I'm sweating out. If I had an idea of what it is like, it wouldn't be so bad. It's this sitting around and waiting that bothers me. Just waiting for tomorrow, and then for the day after, and meanwhile the rain falls harder and you are not a bit closer to flying than you were the first day."

"Oh, well," Macon said, "those are the hardships that you have to contend with. You should have been here when it was rough, though. It really was rough then."

"Oh, nuts," Lloyd said, from behind his book.

"Who pulled your chain?" Macon said.

"Don't worry, Weaver," Lloyd said. "You'll fly soon enough and once they do start scheduling you regularly you'll wonder when the hell they're going to let up on you."

"It's just that I'm wondering what that first one will be like," Weaver said.

"Worrying about it won't help at all," Lloyd said.

"I know that," Weaver said. "I know that, but I'm just wondering what it will be like. I'm *curious*, you know what I mean?" He began to pace the dirt floor. The rain dripped in through five definite holes and Weaver detoured around them as he

49

walked. "Gee, I've never sweated anything out like this in my life."

"What did the supply sergeant say about Buck's stuff?" Lloyd asked, putting his book aside. "The vultures have picked it clean, I guess he can send it out now."

"I was just talking to him," Weaver said. "He asked me to finish packing it and he'd be over tomorrow to pick it up. He said there was a big backlog on that stuff."

Lloyd got to his feet and went over to the orange crate that had been Buck's. "Not much here to pack," he said. "Toilet articles, a can of tooth powder, shoe polish . . ." He began tossing the things into the B-4 bag that he had dragged from under the bed.

"I'll never know why he had shoe polish," Macon said. "There wasn't even anybody around here interested enough in it to swipe it."

"I don't know why anybody would need a shoeshine in this mud," Weaver said.

"Here's a picture of Buck's wife," Lloyd said. He picked up the leather-framed six-by-eight portrait. "She's lovely," he said, admiring it.

"Let's see that," Macon said, taking the picture. "Boy, what a sharp-looking dish. I'd sure like to take her address and look her up when I get back to the States."

"The good die young," Lloyd said flatly to Weaver. "This bastard here will probably live to be a hundred," he nodded toward Macon.

"Okay, wise guy," Macon said, "I won't help you pack that stuff then; *you* do it yourself. I'll watch."

"You're such a big help anyway, fella," Lloyd said. "I don't know what we'd do without you."

Macon laughed. He buttoned up his jacket and ducked out of the tent.

The rain had stopped for the moment and off to his right, at the edge of the street, a six-by-six truck was unloading a pile of 2" x 8" lumber. Brownie, Goodman, Michelson, O'Toole, Flipowitz, Potts and a handful of other men were helping the truck's crew stack the wood on the top of the bank. The ingredients of a Quonset hut lay stacked at the top of the small incline. It's assembly had already begun.

"Come on, Make," Captain Michelson called. "How about a hand here?"

Being thus paged by the Squadron commander, Macon felt trapped. He shrugged wearily and started through the mud, praying for rain as he went.

"It's lumber for the club," O'Toole said, from behind an open-faced grin. "It's for the bar!" O'Toole, Irish as Mrs. Murphy's chowder, was a tall, thin Bostonian, with a button nose and a chin that was as broad as his A's. His curly black hair was matted down with rainwater and his smile narrowed his blue eyes, opened his humor so thoroughly that his grin was infectious. "There's only a few left, Make," he laughed. "You came along just in time."

"I'm synchronized, fella," Macon said, as he joined the group. "Where'd we get the lumber, Mike."

"Tsk, tsk," Captain Michelson laughed. "Silly boy."

"Does Macy's tell Gimbels?" O'Toole said.

"Oh, that's okay then," Macon said. "I was just a little afraid that we *hadn't* stolen it."

Potts and Flipowitz brought up the last pieces and the truck moved off. Willow, a first lieutenant, the supply officer, appeared with some hammers, two saws and a bag full of nails.

"What's the rush?" Macon asked O'Toole. "I hope you jokers aren't getting hysterical about this bar. We can drink all the whiskey we've got now on the sandbars."

"Oh, no," O'Toole laughed. "Leave me clue you up, fella. We're getting some old-fashioned rum shipped in from Manila. The Fat Cat Group is there now. We've also got some coke syrup coming and this Saturday the Squadron is throwing a big, hairy, sloppy party—and there will be women!"

"Easy kid," Macon said, from behind a look of shock. "This sun is getting to you."

"No stuff, Make," O'Toole said. "Some nurses and some civilian volunteer workers from down near Naha are coming. Brownie knows one of the volunteers and she's bringing along her play-mates."

"Oh, ecstasy," Macon said. "Women; and white, too. Aren't they?"

"Yeah, that's the ungarbled word that I got," O'Toole said. "And do you remember when we were in San Antonio that nurse I met from Brooks General? I just found out that she's here, too. She's also bringing her playmates."

"Cozy. What was her name again?"

"Caddie Hamilton," O'Toole said.

"Oh, yes; say, Oatie, she was okay."

"I know. I know," O'Toole said. "The Fat Cat is due back on Friday, so the stuff will be under guard until the party."

"That's acceptable," Macon said. "But who's

going to watch the guard?" The Fat Cat was a C-47, named the 'Angel of Mercy' that belonged to the Group and performed these and similar missions. It occurred to Macon that this was probably the most merciful jaunt to date.

The work had begun in earnest. Flipowitz and Potts were sawing, Michelson and Goodman were hammering, and Willow was arguing with everyone about what should be done about it. Things were, Macon concluded, under control.

CHAPTER V

Saturday, 28 July trudged into the 606th Bombardment Squadron in answer to the perspiring anticipation of the small group of men who had conceived for it an importance far out of proportion on an island where war came to call in Jap Bettys every night.

The party at the club had taken top billing any time two of them met. They had awaited it with bated pangs of nervous excitement and upon its arrival, even the moon came out periodically to watch. Scattered clouds, as always, held the threat of sudden rain, but the men disregarded the ominous signs and went all out—clean khakis were eased out of cramped B-4 bags and shoe brushes made furious attempts to erase the caked muck. The open-air shower had swarmed with jabbering men all afternoon and much shaving lather had passed into the Okinawa mud by the time eight o'clock came by.

Macon left the tent at a few minutes past the hour. This was no time for dramatic entrance, he decided. The women would be occupied within fifteen minutes after their arrival. He picked his way carefully through the mire on tip-toe, walking as daintily as his size eleven low-cut shoes would tolerate. He didn't have too much trouble getting there, the journey was quite short. The club stood at the east end of the officer's area, atop the small incline above the street. The building looked agog with lights, a few of the men had gotten there earlier. It was a half-breed building, half Quonset hut and half wood-and-tarpaulin. The top had patches of steel matting, dabs of canvas. The floor was of wood.

Macon went in, jammed his flight cap into his raincoat pocket, tossed the coat onto the corner of the Ping-Pong table that had been shoved there for just that purpose. The club, in its finished state, presented a picture of comfort and cleanliness that was grossly exaggerated in this land of mud. It had a floor, and fairly comfortable seats, and even had two homemade reading lamps. The value could never be overestimated. The door that had admitted Macon into the northwest corner deposited him in the lounge. The collection of varied and nondescript furniture pieces—fourteen chairs and three crude tables—were rationed to the various parts of the room and showed to the fullest advantage. The reading lamps had cautiously disappeared. A hint of a partition hypothetically divided the building into two equal rooms—the bar and the lounge. The bar itself controlled a healthy one-quarter of that room, for it was complete with its attentive chairs and stools. A long bench nestled against the opposite wall.

O'Toole came in, Macon watched him from the

bench in the bar. He also left his coat on the broad, green table near the door, came in behind a broad smile, sat down. "What say, fella." He lit a cigarette. "When does the bar open?"

"Beats the hell out of me, Oatie," Macon said. "I just got here myself."

"I guess they decided not to slop up the refreshments until the women come. Sounds like a tolerable idea, though," O'Toole said. He settled back against one of the few wooden planks in the side of the building, crossed his legs, took a long drag on his cigarette. "They were due to get here at eight; but here it is eight-twenty and I'm early. Guess maybe the mud's quite bad, though."

They sat in silence for nearly five minutes, watching some of the other men arrive. Captain Brown and Captain Michelson came in together and sat in the lounge. Pop Goodman came over to check with the two corporals who were tending bar. He had arranged for the club to procure some extra ice from the 659th and he was probably checking on it.

They heard Willow before they saw him, which was per usual. His voice far exceeded all else about him, and that left much to be desired. Macon did not like him and as was his pleasure he had on various choice occasions allowed the impression to circulate. Now Willow didn't care for him either. In fact, they spoke only when Macon was wanting badly enough to swallow his pride in exchange for supplies, and Macon had squandered much time on numerous necessities while waiting to catch the supply sergeant in charge. Willow wasn't, Macon was positive, actually very popular in general. This is what had provoked Macon's dislike and pleasure;

it made him feel as though he was speaking for all the boys every time he said something unkind to Willow. There was no doubt that the men became uncomfortable in the club in Willow's presence, for his escapades were well-remembered but ill-famed; he had the unhappy knack of becoming excessively and mournfully self-confessing concerning his own plight and almost always concluded his evening with considerable wailing and weeping and nearly always by challenging someone to a fight. He had the uncomfortable faculty of being what is distastefully referred to as a 'sloppy drunk.' The men called him 'Weeping' Willow. No one disputed it.

Willow had a small head with close-cropped hair, a wide undernourished mustache. He began talking to Brown and Michelson just about the time the G.I. bus, that usually carried them to the flight line for mission, slid to a muddy halt in the road outside. A few minutes later over a half-a-dozen girls of varying shapes, sizes and degrees of beauty came jabbering into the lounge and as if produced by magic, nearly every other man in the Squadron came charging in behind them. It was like a treasure hunt.

Macon grabbed a slight brunette before she had had a chance to slip out of her raincoat. He practically stripped her of it while telling her about the terrible weather they were having. "Wasn't it terrible?" he said. He took her arm, guided her toward the bar.

"Rush Macon's my name," he said, displaying the broadest smile he'd felt need of in a long time. "My friends call me Make, but I don't care for it."

She was rather pretty, in a plain sort of way. Brown eyes wrinkled when she smiled and white

57

teeth sparkled when her thin lips parted. She had a pretty chin, a neat up-on-the-sides-down-in-the-back hairdo. Wearing a spotless, well-tailored uniform of a Civilian Volunteer Organization, she looked neat as a pin; Macon was well-pleased. "Virginia," she said. "Virginia Weldon."

"You'll never know what meeting you has done for my morale, really," he said. "This place definitely needs the patter of female feet."

She smiled gracefully, said nothing. He wondered if she spoke the language, decided that she must, tried again.

"How about a drink?" They were nearly to the bar by then, so both his question and her answer could be deftly excluded from the realm of clever repartée.

"All right," she said.

He got two drinks, deposited the required ten yen, led her to a corner of the lounge. They were early enough to get two chairs, fairly comfortable and side-by-side.

"What do you do with yourself on this godfor-saken island?" he asked. "I can ask that of you with an absolutely clear conscience, because you volunteered. At least, that's what they say to the jokers around here who joined. I really don't know if it's fair, really—but it does make conversation."

"It isn't bad," she explained. "We're kept pretty busy. There's lots to do."

"There's no doubt about that," he said.

They spoke of his Squadron and he explained how they ran off a strafing mission, and she was genuinely interested and fascinated. They spoke of her job and she told him how she enjoyed visiting the hospitals and how wonderful the wounded and sick men were, and he tried keenly to look interested. They talked of home and she reminisced about her home in Michigan and about her school; they spoke of the war; they spoke of Okinawa; they spoke of nothing very vital. By ten o'clock they were in the throes of their fourth drink, and he was rushing her along into the subjects that he wanted discussed as quickly and as subtly as he could manage.

They danced to the music of a battered Victrola and to the undulant rhythms of the club's radio, a wayward airplane radio mounted in a small ammunition box. It had been "Bull" Jones', but he had been killed at Leyte. Macon held her close. He hadn't held anyone like her for such a long time. They danced and joked and he held her tight when the music was right.

It was at about ten-thirty, during their fifth drink, that the air raid sirens began heralding their nightly message. Macon surpressed a smile—those damn Japs certainly had taken their time about arriving!

Lights were disappearing quickly, the men weren't wasting a minute. Macon got to one of the lights first, he gingerly clicked the cord. When he returned he drew his chair closer to Virginia's.

"These air raids were terribly exciting at first," she said, "but now they are getting to be an awful nuisance."

"This is the first time I've enjoyed one," he laughed. He put his arm about the back of her chair. "See?" he cooed, "you've changed my viewpoint on the whole war already."

She laughed; laughed like she didn't believe him, but wanted him to keep saying things like that.

"You have, really. I think that it is a serious

matter, and you shouldn't laugh it off so lightly."

"I wasn't making fun," she said, "really I wasn't, Rush."

"I'm glad," he said. "Do you know, Ginny, you're by far the nicest thing that's happened to me in a long time."

"How long have you been overseas?" There was mischief in her smile.

"There you go again. You just won't take me seriously, will you?"

"Yes," she said.

"Well, I'm not just making up conversation to pass the time of day, or to sell you a bill of goods. I'm having such a wonderful time here tonight, with you, and everything is well, well . . ."

"What, Rush?"

"Oh, never mind," he said. "I don't want to say anything that would give you the impression that I'm handing you a line."

"Please don't feel that way about it, Rush. I don't think you are—really I don't."

"That's good," he said. His arm went about her shoulders, brought her closer. He bent over her face to kiss her.

"No, Rush; don't," she said.

He recoiled his arm quickly to his side. "Okay, okay," he said. "I don't know how else I can impress you with the fact that I like you!"

"But," she said, "but, you just met me . . ."

"But, hell. If you're really interested in what I think, I'll tell you how I feel about the whole deal."

"Tell me," she said. "You know that I'm very interested."

"I don't believe in kissing for kissing alone. I gave up trying to kiss all the girls on the block when

I was a young kid. The idea of kissing just-for-the-record is kid's stuff. I believe that kissing is merely a means of conveying some emotion—if it's utilized correctly. My trying to kiss you just then only illustrated that I wanted to display affection. I hope I don't sound as though I'm trying to be too profound, because what I want to say is just that, that, well, you're refusing to kiss me, just sort of left us in a blind alley."

"What do you mean?" She was interested enough, and looked just puzzled enough.

He conceded that he was good, bent a bit closer to her. "Well, the failure of two people to kiss has happened, probably, more times than has their kissing. What I mean is, when they don't kiss they fail to establish a common ground for future meetings. When they have kissed, they meet again, kiss again, and they are ready to pick up where they left off. With us, now, we have no common ground established. If we were to meet again, we would have to start all over again, because, actually, we've gone nowhere."

"I, ah . . ."

"It's just this," he said. "If nothing out-of-the-ordinary happens tonight, you know that the possibilities of our having a date in the immediate future are slim. Right?"

"I don't think so," she said thoughtfully. "If you wanted to see me again you . . ."

"What encouragement have you given me?" He leaned still closer to her face.

"I had hoped that I had given you enough; enough to make you want to see me again."

"Do you want me to see you again?" His arm moved about the back of her chair.

"Yes I do."

He leaned forward and she lifted her face slightly. Her lips were warm and a quiver ran through her body and into his arm that had brought her close to him. He kissed her again, softly, teasing her parted lips until her right arm went about his neck and pulled him within range. She kissed him hard.

"You're awfully nice," he said. "I think you're swell."

She smiled and nestled against his shoulder. "I'm glad," she said.

He kissed her lightly on the nose. "Do you want a cigarette, honey?" He gave her one, took one himself and lit them both. For the first time since the air raid began he became conscious of the presence of other people, of the sound of the guns. The club had become quieter now, the bar was still operating, but the building was semi-deserted. A few couples danced to the music of the Victrola. Somebody was kissing somebody else over in the other corner.

"What did you do before?" she asked. "Before you got into the army, I mean."

"Oh, different things, I guess. None of them much good, though," he said. "And I didn't care very much about them."

"Tell me?"

"Well, let's see," he said, trying to mold some reality into what now seemed merely a dream. "When I got out of high school, I worked in the stock room in a department store. I worked there for about a year, then I got a promotion—right into the cellar; I became head man in charge of the basement stock room. Then, after a while, I quit. I worked in a haberdashery shop for a couple of months, then I got a job in a ship-yard. That's all, I guess."

"Did you have any college?"

"I went to night school for about a year and a half. Oh, I was a real eager beaver. Yes sir, real eager beaver."

"There's ah, one thing," she said, hesitatingly, "I've been sort of wondering about."

"No, I'm not married," he laughed.

She laughed too. "I'm glad. I'm glad you're not married."

"Do you know what?" he said.

"What?"

"You're too far away from me. What are you doing way over there? Here, come on over." He leaned out, took her hands, gently pulled her toward where he was sitting, pulled her down on his lap. He gazed about him in the darkness. He was proud of this last manoeuvre. He put his arms about her and kissed her and held her tightly against him; her body slid part-way around toward him. Her arms were about his neck and he kissed her daintily again, and again. Eyes closed, her head rested on his shoulder. She seemed very contented. He kissed her, hard, and his hand found its way away from her waist, up under her arm to her breast. She flinched, pushed his hand away.

"Don't," she said.

"I'm sorry. I didn't think I was doing anything wrong."

"Please be nice."

"I'm always as nice as I know how to be," he laughed. He couldn't say more for she silenced him by lowering her head and kissing him.

63

A deep, female voice interrupted them somewhat later. It was the voice of an older woman, and she spoke with authority. She was summoning the civilian volunteer workers to prepare to leave. The air raid was over, she was saying, and it was getting late and they had a long way to go and the roads were very bad and they had to get sleep to be able to get up for work the next day.

Macon withdrew his hand from beneath her blouse, she quickly straightened it. "Why couldn't we have gotten someone drunk enough to take care of that old bag," he said.

She laughed half-aloud, kissed him quickly. The lights were reappearing. "I wish that I was a nurse; I'd be able to stay longer," she said.

"I certainly hate to see you go," he said. "When can I see you again?"

She was explaining to him exactly where on the island she lived, and worked, and how he could get in touch with her when the older woman's voice blurted out again. She was oldish, heavy with years, rather pleasant-looking, but Macon thought she talked too much and too loudly.

"You don't ever just happen to have one of those ambulances of yours out for a joyride sometimes?" he laughed. "Up in this direction, I mean?"

The girls were climbing into their raincoats. Macon walked with Virginia to the door, took her coat from the rack, helped her into it.

"Do you think there might be a chance?" he asked. "You see, it's pretty hard to get hold of a jeep around here."

"Call me tomorrow," she said softly. "I think I might be able to fix it up." She kissed him quickly, followed the others out.

64

Nearly a dozen nurses, stationed only a handful of miles away from the area, were still present as Macon recalled his attention from the departing bus. He went to the bar, ordered a drink, lit a cigarette. He watched the dancers and the two couples making love in the semi-darkness of the lounge, snorted at one of the more familiar sights— Willow weeping into his rum.

Some time and some drinks later he crushed the cigarette that he happened to have at hand, slid from the stool, moved to the door, dragged his raincoat from the Ping-Pong table, slipped it on. It wasn't until he stepped outside and attempted to pick his way through the mud that he realized that he was quite drunk. His feet were insubordinate and he went splashing ungracefully through the area. He turned, ducked into a darkened tent that looked exactly like every other darkened tent in the vicinity, stumbled blindly across a dirt floor, kicked a chair—someone had moved in a new floor while he was away; Macon wondered who could have done that. He caught his foot on some solidly nailed planks, and he lunged toward the faintly visible bed in the corner, his protective hands thrust searchingly out in front of him. He landed directly on top of a man's prone body. Macon began to unravel as quickly as his unsteady hands could free him; he looked down at the back of Brownie's neck.

Macon required a long, embarrassed, alcoholic moment to lift his weight from the captain's back, push himself away and divorce his grip from the squirming man. Macon was about to speak apologetically when a woman's voice came up to him from the darkness below.

"Thanks." That was all she said.

65

CHAPTER VI

Macon, Weaver and Lloyd had just returned from Sunday morning breakfast when Captain Brown came in, blinking and bleary-eyed.

"Well, good morning," Lloyd said. "And how is every little thing on this fine, rainy morning?"

"Not good. Not very good at all," Brown said, patting the side of his head gently. "I'm not feeling very keen."

"Drink and women," Macon laughed. "Drink and women will lead a man to his doom every time. I read that someplace."

"Hmmm," Lloyd said.

"But what a way to get yourself doomed," Macon said.

"You weren't doing badly yourself," Lloyd said to Macon. "You were certainly snowing that poor little girl that you had in tow."

"You know, Make," Brownie said, "there's something that has been bothering me all morning. I dreamt that I saw you come into the tent and try to roll me out of bed. Seems very odd to me why I should dream anything like that but it stands out so clearly in my mind. . . ."

"That was no dream, buddy, " Macon said. He laughed. "It wasn't the *bed* I rolled you out of, either. Besides, I didn't realize what I was doing, Brownie, or I wouldn't have been so damn inquisitive; honest I wouldn't. . . ."

"Oh."

"Well, I will say," Macon said, continuing, "you had all the comforts of home away from home—lampooning a scragg right in your own front room!"

"It never happened," Brown said flippantly. "Well, I've got to go fly the kinks out of a new engine. There doesn't seem to be anyone else up to it around here today." He went out.

"I'm a fatalist," Weaver said, "but he's overdoing it a little; flying with a hangover like that."

"Being fatalistic has nothing to do with it," Macon said.

Weaver eyed Macon carefully. "What do you mean?"

"Oh, boy; here we go again," Lloyd said.

"If you can fly the plane and if the plane is in good shape, being fatalistic has nothing to do with it at all."

"Why a million things can happen in an airplane," Weaver said, protesting.

"But there are the basic facts alone that are important," Macon said, with authority dripping from his voice. "It's merely the mechanics of flying and the construction of your airplane that count."

"How do you account for one guy, say, in a crew getting shot-up while nobody else gets touched?" Weaver asked impatiently.

"Fate *may* play its little part," Macon said, "but

I doubt it seriously. It depends on where you put the airplane at that particular second."

"But we do things like that instinctively," Weaver said. "We don't do things like that carefully. Even you will have to admit that—that we do things that seem to be motivated by something greater than ourselves. Isn't that true?"

"Please don't get him started, Weaver," Lloyd said. "He gives this same line of theory and sawdust to everybody. Even if he doesn't believe it himself."

"I believe whatever I say, damn it," Macon said quickly. "I say that fate or religion, or whatever you want to call it, hasn't got a damn thing to do with whether you hang your jock."

"Well, what *do* you believe in then?" Weaver said.

"I believe in the Wright Engine and the Browning .50 Calibre Machine Gun. They are the power that is keeping this Group going, and anybody who says they aren't is a hypocrite. They are the symbol of the power that we feel in ourselves." Macon lit a cigarette; this sort of argument stimulated him. "However, if you fly with your head up your ass, though, I will admit that you probably won't get home."

"That's all you believe in?" Weaver demanded. "The more mechanical things that we use—and you have no regard for anything else?"

"Like what?"

"Religion, or . . . or the Bible."

"Oh," Macon said, "I respect them all right; I just don't take them too seriously."

"I warned you, Weaver," Lloyd said.

"You believe in just the Wright Engine and the

Browning Machine Gun," Weaver said, as if toyfully bouncing the thought about in his mind.

"I believe in science," Macon said. "I believe that everything eminates from the atom and the electron; not from the heart. Everything we've got has a sound, scientific basis and a logical theory behind it—it can be explained—explained and demonstrated very logically and very coldly."

"What do you mean?"

"I mean that it involved no miracle from heaven to bring us this far in the war. Nothing Almighty struck down the Germans. Nothing divine is going to knock out the Japs. It will be guns and ships and planes and you can find the blueprints for every damn one of them if you look hard enough—it's all down in black and white!"

"Don't you believe in religion at all?" Weaver said.

"I believe in science. Science has the answer for everything."

"Did you ever read the Bible?"

"Yes, and I've read *Forever Amber*, too," Macon said. "But I take them both with a grain of salt. I put more faith in history—that's a true record of the accomplishments of man; it tells how man is where he is; it tells why we have a democracy and why airplanes fly and why women have miscarriages. Why, it even gives you a good idea of what to expect in the future. No amount of faith will do that." Macon paced the floor. "No amount of praying averted this war, and heaven knows we prayed hard enough; but, it was history that explained the story to us, not your neighborhood Bible School."

"The Bible is history," Weaver said. "If it isn't

history, I don't know what is! It traces the story of religion and the development of man's thoughts—"

"Nuts," Macon said. "It's religious propaganda; that's all it is. At best, it's the views and opinions of a relatively small group of men. A small group of men who were impressed by what they felt—which is only natural, I suppose. History, on the other hand, is as authentic as anything can be—we only have to look around us to see the results of the history lesson that we failed to prepare. It is very possible to prove history's worth. But you can't show me much proof for the statements made in the Bible—like the Red Sea's parting, for instance. If you can, I'll start going to church today."

"There are many, many things in the Bible that are just as true today as they were when they were written," Weaver said. "Also, we know that there must have been a beginning. In order to imagine that beginning, we have to believe just what they tell us—what else is there to believe? Now, I know you'll say that there is a scientific explanation for everything—but what is right and what is not? Darwin and a lot of others tried to explain it. . . ."

"Osmosis was the beginning, I imagine," Macon said. "I don't claim to know much about the Bible. I did my biblical reading in Sunday School—and they *made* me go there."

"The Bible is a great comfort, I think," Weaver said. "When you feel the need of strength, and of faith. . . ."

"Now hold on," Macon said. "Don't tell me that those jokers who suddenly find themselves getting shot at and who start praying like mad because they haven't another damn thing to do anyway— don't tell me *they* are religious! They're hypocrites,

70

that's all they are!"

"Religion, as far as I can see," said Weaver, "is heart-felt. If you feel it you have it. A man isn't pious just because he goes to church every week; because he could go out right after and commit a sin. But, he's got to feel religion in his heart and in his conscience. He has to feel the simple, humble things. . . ."

"I've heard of too many humble and simple people stealing their neighbor's chickens or committing rape on some little kid," Macon said, with a snort. "The simpler they are, the worse they seem to be."

"That's too stupid an observation to waste time talking about," Weaver said. "But I'll tell you something about your comparison of science to religion. The scientist has found ways of keeping parts of the body alive—he has even frozen living things, thereby killing them—then he has made them live again. That is truly magnificent. The scientist can create a man, I imagine, from the necessary ingredients—and the man that they would construct would probably be able to walk and talk and drink scotch—but the scientist will never make it into a human being. He can't because he can't give his man a soul. Science will never be that precise. There will always be that something about nature that will just surpass the scientist's best efforts."

"Now wait a minute. . . ." Macon said. "We were discussing how the board of directors in charge of crimes and punishment would send violators down to hell to shovel some coal before being admitted by Saint Peter. You know, like being on detached service in Hades for awhile."

"If you can tell me how science can create a mind and a soul for a man, perhaps that will answer your silly arguments," Weaver said.

"Well," Macon said, "I am a firm believer in the theory that you should never argue with a man about his religion or his taste in women. Personally, I believe in the scientist and think he'll invent or discover anything he feels he needs badly enough. But . . . I'm tolerant; you can believe in the Bible, or whatever else you want to; I don't mind." He got up from his cot, walked over to the tent door. "And I won't even tell the guys that a new man in the Squadron was popping off in here." He went out.

He crossed over to the Orderly Room. There was a corporal reading at one of the back tables. Otherwise the tent looked deserted, even for a Sunday.

He picked up the field telephone. He rang Council Exchange. Council Exchange got him Cockerel Exchange. Cockerel Exchange connected him with Drake Exchange. It was a robust fifteen minutes later when he finally spoke to the Naha Exchange and got the number he requested.

"Miss Virginia Weldon, please."

"Hello."

"Virginia?" he said. "This is Macon."

"Oh, oh, Rush." She sighed a little, laughed a little. "I've been waiting for your call all morning. How are you? Did you sleep well? You didn't have a hangover this morning, I hope."

"Wait a minute," he laughed. "Wait a minute. One thing at a time."

"Oh, I'm sorry. Guess I'm a little excited."

"How did you make out on that transportation deal, Angel," he said. "Any luck?"

"I guess that's what really topped off my excitement, Rush. Yes, I have permission to use a vehicle. Bet you'll never guess what it is?"

"A boa constrictor?"

"No; silly," she laughed deeply. ' ı got permiss' ɔn to take an *ambulance*. Miss Watkins is letting me use hers."

"Who?"

"You know, the woman wıo was in charge of us last night?" she said. "The one that you were sorry wasn't with someone. . . ."

"Oh, yes; yes indeed. Cute," he said.

"It was very nice of her, I think."

"Well," he said, "you'll be coming to call in style. Have you ever driven one before? I'd certainly hate to have you hang your—er, ah; have any trouble with the thing—they're, they're rather bulky, you know."

"Oh, I've driven them often," she said. "The only thing I'm concerned about is the route to get there; but I suppose I can get it from one of the regular drivers."

"What's that? Oh, the *route*!" He laughed like someone appreciating his own humor to the fullest. The corporal at the rear table eyed him curiously. "I guess I was thinking about a couple of other things," Macon said.

"Slap your mind," she said. There was a smile in her voice, a tone of amusement. He was glad that she wasn't displeased. Nothing ventured, nothing gained. He flicked his cigarette out through the door of the tent.

"When will you be able to make it, Angel?" he said.

"Well, I finish work at five o'clock," she said. "I should be able to make it by eight."

"When you finish, charge out of the shop, change your girdle, and taxi on over. It gets dark at a few minutes to eight, and—ahh, well," he laughed. "It's hard to find your way after dark." He laughed some more. The corporal shook his head doubtfully. "Besides, I've scrounged a couple of bottles of beer for the big party. The longer we wait, the warmer they get—and they're pretty warm right now."

"I'll hurry, I promise," she said.

"See you then," he said.

"Okay, honey," she said. " 'Bye."

He signed off by ringing the crank, hung the phone back on its nail, lit a cigarette, glanced at the corporal, and went out. The corporal smiled a little, nodded approval.

CHAPTER VII

It was still raining a steady, dreary rain as an ambulance pulled up in front of the Orderly Room, and a raincoated figure got into the front seat.

"You're late," Macon said. "Did you have any trouble?" He slipped out of his coat, folded it over his arm, reached into the side pockets to produce six bottles of beer. He displayed them as though they were prize fish that he had just caught.

"No," she was saying, "I only got lost twice." Then she noticed the beer. "Oh, all the comforts of home."

"I had to kill off four jokers to get this booty," he laughed. "I even had to do some borrowing on next week's ration."

"How much do you get?"

"Six warm bottles per week per man—provided, of course, the ship comes in. In the happen stance that it doesn't—then we get six warm beers every *two* weeks."

She laughed. She looked very pretty—casually cute, he observed. She wore a blouse that looked to him like a cross between a sweatshirt and a sweater—it had long sleeves, a v-neck, and in its snugness she looked rounder and fuller than she had in her uniform the night before. She wore slacks of blue that seemed quite compatible with the blouse of white. Her hair was slightly mussed—not too mussed—it looked rather homey and comfortable to Macon.

"I don't make a practice of coming to call on my dates," she said. "In fact, the more I thought about the idea, the less I liked it. I've never done it before, I don't even know the procedure." She had started the vehicle and was shifting into second, moving slowly over the bumpy, slippery road.

"Well," he said slowly, watching her carefully, "first you talk about the weather or something as unimportant—to break the ice. You know, you've got to get the person you're calling on in the mood for whatever you want that person to be in the mood for."

"But what if I don't have ulterior motives?"

"You've got to have something in mind," he said. "Otherwise you're standing still; and you know what they say about standing still in the face of progress?"

"Yes."

"Then you tell me how cute I look in my slightly soiled khakis and my 1945 model A-2 jacket, leather, field, brown. And you rave about my new, daintily preserved hat—complete with the 78 mission crush. And, of course, you must comment—favorably, naturally, about my Channel No. 36. You know, make me think you appreciate all the trouble I went through to make myself desirable for you. . . ."

"Well, I *do*, dearie; I *do*." She laughed. "You're simply fetching."

"That's it," he said, gaily. "Tell me how nice I look—you know, that you think I look simply ravishing."

She laughed. "You nut," she said.

"Then, if you don't know much about the countryside, you ask—subtly, of course—about a nice quiet spot at which we can partake of aforementioned beer."

"Do I have to?"

"No, but you should. And I would feel hurt and neglected if you didn't."

"You wouldn't—not *too* hurt." It was hard to tell just what she *was* thinking.

"Well, you know the old axiom," he said, "a girl will forgive you for a kiss that you took when you shouldn't have, but she'll never forgive you for not taking a kiss that you should have."

She drove on in silence. They bumped and slid along the uneven ruts. They began to leave the Group area behind them and the road dipped off the hill. She stopped, shifted into low, started down very slowly. The ambulance seemed to be moving cautiously, continually putting a tire out to feel its way. The road appeared to be no more than a small creek that couldn't decide which rut it was going to sleep in. The wheels of the vehicle couldn't decide anything, either.

"There's a big coral quarry over here to the right," he said. "And there is a neat little revetment for us to toss old, used beer bottles over."

"I really don't think we should, Rush."

"Well, okay—that is, if you can drink your beer and drive at the same time. I don't think that I should

77

have given you all that whiskey last night; I spoiled you for the commonplace pleasures. I think you're getting out of the warm beer class. Next thing I know you'll be expecting *cold* beer."

She smiled.

"Do you realize, young lady, the terrifically high premium that ice commands around here? It's harder to get than discharge points. It's much harder to get, in fact, than the beer is." He lit two cigarettes, stuck one in her mouth as she drove. She nodded, still trying to pick her way along the imitation road. The rain hitting the windshield made her task more difficult.

"Next road to the right," he said. She said nothing. They skidded out of the deep grooves that were the road, but he reached over and helped give the wheel a hard yank and they slid back on course.

At the corner she turned right, followed his directions to the far left corner of the wide area. Darkness all but concealed the monstrous grating and sifting machine that crushed the coral and assorted the pieces according to size. She swung around, backed against the high wall of the huge quarry. There were dirt and coral banks on three sides climbing to approximately twenty to twenty-five feet. Only the side through which they had entered was flat and straight-away. She left the gears in reverse, turned off the ignition, pushed off the lights.

"There, are you happy now?" She seemed displeased.

"Well, yes; now that you mention it." He rolled the window down, flicked out his cigarette. "But that's not the way you do it. You park, turn out the lights, put your arm around me and coyly say, 'Oops, must have run out of gas!'" He held out two bottles of beer. "Then you suggest that while we're waiting for the garageman to come and change the damn tire, we might as well drink these beers that you just happened to have along."

She rolled down her window, dropped her cigarette out. He still couldn't tell if she was happy.

"Then, of course," he said, "you could begin to tell me how lovely you thought my eyes were and how you'd like to take me out of all this, this coral and dishwater; take me away from the pool room. You know, trial and error—realizing, of course, that sooner or later I would succumb to your fatal charm and fly away with you to your little bamboo shack atop Fujiyama."

"Oh, you're silly." That was a little better.

"Or, you could tell me what a miserable life you've had since you had to give up the B-29 and move into that filthy old B-25; playing on my sympathy, of course. And, you could suggest we drink some warm beer so that you could drown your sorrows and punish yourself at one and the same time." He studied her. "Get the picture?"

"Okay, okay," she laughed, "I surrender. I surrender. Let's drink one of those beers, if it will make you any happier."

"No, no' it's supposed to make *you* happier. But, I'm convinced; I'm convinced that you're drinking just so that I won't be forced to drink alone. For you realize all the time, of course, that not many people care for the practice of drinking alone; unless, naturally, they are characters of ill-breeding and ill-mannered manners."

Virginia laughed. "You're priceless, you nut. You're

79

far and away out of this world."

"No, no; in that case you're supposed to say, 'are you free tonight, baby?—and I coyly reply that I'm not free, but I'm very reasonable."

Her gaiety again seemed in doubt. He opened two beers, gave her one, took a swig of his. "Hmmmm, that's good," he said, "even if it is on the tepid side."

"It is good."

"That's it; that's it—you're doing fine. Now the object is to get me drunk. That's the target for tonight."

"I think you're utterly impossible." She laughed and drank some beer.

By the end of the first bottle of beer she seemed to be in much better spirits. After the second their conversation was tinted with happy, easy humor, for warm beer and gay hearts functioned together like two Wright Engines. Half-way through the last brew he grasped the happy conclusion that they were merely sitting there drinking themselves into a drunken state. He yearned for about four more bottles.

She was saying that she had had a light supper and she wondered if the beer would affect her more severely because of it, or did he think the warm weather had anything to do with it?

"Oh, no," he said, with a magnanimous wave of the hand. "It won't bother you at all. In fact, it will supply you with all the vitamins that you didn't get for supper."

"Oh," she said.

"Come on, Angel, bottoms up; let's drink 'er down!" He began to sing a drinking song, "Here's to u-s, we're true blue; we are drunkards thru and

80

thru. We are drunkards, people say—meant to go to heaven but we went the other way, so drink, chug-a-lug, chug-a-lug, chug-a-lug; so drink, chug-a . . ." and he was lost in the swim of disposing of his own beer.

She drank also, with bottle tipped up; she drank in small, steady swallows and when she had finished she sat quietly excited and sighed. "My, my."

"Good, wasn't it?" he said, tossing his bottle out of the window. He took hers and threw it out also. "Boy, I wish we had some more."

"I think I'm just as happy we haven't another drop," she said slowly. "I'm just as happy. I'd like to sit here and think it over for a minute or two, and inhale all this nice, fresh, hot air." Her voice sounded strange.

"Are you all right?" he said. He moved over to her, put an arm about her shoulders, leaned forward to look into her face. "You okay?"

"Oh, sure. Drinking warm beer really isn't anything new around here. In fact, drinking cold beer would probably be a shock to my system. I'm just about used to warm beer. I *like* cold beer, you understand. But, warm beer is nice."

"I certainly do agree," he said, looking into her face.

"I thought you would," she smiled, "there's nothing really wrong with warm beer at all—that some ice won't fix—especially if you have cold beer. Warm beer has loads of vitamins, too."

"You're so right, Angel. Lots of vitamins."

"Yes sir; lots of them. Big ones, and little ones, and oh, just lots of them."

"Vitamins?"

"Hmmmmm."

"You're right, Angel. You're right as rabbits." He looked into her eyes, they were a little glassy, but he didn't believe that she was actually drunk. However, it might take a few minutes for her to shake off that last, long one. That idea of drinking bottoms-up was rough, especially when you weren't used to it; he was delighted to discover that she wasn't used to it.

"Gee, honey," she said, finally, "you shouldn't make me drink like we drank that last bottle; it isn't good for me."

"Whatta' drinker," he laughed. "But you're recovery is good."

"Mmmmmm."

"Are you happy, Angel? Glad you came?"

"Mmmmmmmmmm," she smiled and patted his face once with her hand, held his chin gently. "Yes, I'm terribly glad."

He bent forward and kissed her. Her arms went about him and she held him tightly. Her lips quivered and a tremble seemed to pass through her whole body. He kissed her again and sweeping her into his embrace he pulled her tight against him. Her arms were strong about his neck and his caressing hands moved slowly over her back and hips. Passion seemed to grow within her like flood waters rising in the shower of kisses. He covered her neck and cheeks and lips with full, quick kisses and his hand discovered that she wore no bra under her blouse. Her breasts were round and firm and suddenly she was pushing him away.

"Don't, Rush; don't! Please don't!"

"Can I help it if I want you so much? Can I?"

"But I don't want it to be like this—not like this. I, I . . ."

"I can't help it," he explained sharply. "I can't help it if I want you so badly." He kissed her again, but she eluded him.

"You're just very lonely," she said slowly. "You're letting your head run away with your heart. It's really no compliment to me. . . ."

He drew back, looked at her solemnly. "If that's what you think then we might as well go back. I wouldn't want it to get around that I insulted you by telling you how much I liked you and wanted you." He sat back, displayed his most prized pout.

"I, I—but; but, you don't understand, Rush," she said. "You just don't seem to understand." She seemed to be working very hard with what she was trying to say. "I can't. . . ."

"You can't what?" he said quickly. "You can't *love* me because you *like* me too much—you're afraid to break up this friendship with too much affection—is that it—or what exactly is it that you mean?"

"No, no—I . . ."

"Well, what is it then?"

"Would you marry me?" she said softly.

"Not tomorrow, or the next day. I don't know if I'll still be around next week."

She sat quietly in the corner of the front seat, looking down at her hands as they rested in her lap. He was leaning, left arm first, against the seat next to her right shoulder. He moved away, lit a cigarette, inhaled soberly. The defense rests, he thought.

She did not move or speak until half a cigarette later. "What are you thinking, Rush?"

"About grouse, I guess. Actually, I give up; you're doing the thinking for this outfit."

"Don't be angry; please."

He said nothing, inhaled some more of his cigarette.

"May I have a cigarette?" she said. He gave her one, lit it with a match. "I don't want to be unreasonable," she said slowly. "But, but, I don't exactly know what you expect. I don't even know if you like me. You never said anything about it, you know."

"Certainly I do," he said quickly. "If I didn't seem anxious enough to see you again—if I didn't give you that impression, then I'm sorry. Would I have wanted this date so soon if I didn't like you?" He tossed away the used cigarette. "If you expect me to make pretty speeches, though, I'm sorry to be such a disappointment. I don't relish flowery talk; I like to call a spade a spade."

"What do you mean?"

"I mean that if I said I loved you, you could be damn sure I did love you. If I told you I liked you and wanted you—which I certainly hope you sincerely believe, because I do—then I like you. I won't tell you what isn't true. And anything I do tell you, you can bet your bottom dollar that it's true."

"I'm glad you are that way, Rush. I do want you to be honest with me."

"Yes, and I would like you to be honest with me."

"I try to be."

"Do you?"

"What makes you say it like that?" she looked puzzled.

"I just don't think that you were very honest a little while ago; were you? I think you want me as much as I want you—if that's possible," he said in a hard tone that made her look quickly at him. "All I know is, black is black and white is white—and that's just what they are—neither one of them is grey."

"Oh, Rush," she said, turning to him. "Please don't be angry with me."

He took her shoulders firmly, brought her to him, kissed her lips lustfully. Her arms were about him again and his hands found her hips and brought them to him and held her tight against him and were lost under her blouse and loosened the buttons on the left side of her slacks. Her flesh felt warm and firm and he spoke softly.

"Let's get into the back."

CHAPTER VII

It was just becoming dawn when Macon awoke. The woolen blankets on the ambulance stretcher itched and annoyed his nude body. Virginia was still asleep on his arm with her mussed hair falling on the blanket that he had folded to use as a pillow.

He kissed her pale lips softly, she stirred and opened her eyes. "It's morning, Angel," he said. "These jokers probably come to work early around here."

She bounded to her elbow and he dropped back the blanket. The G.I. stretcher was too narrow for both of them to sit up at the same time. He lay on the outside, half off as it were.

She put her arm about his waist. "Careful, honey, don't fall."

"I won't," he said.

She leaned over and kissed him, her breasts felt heavy on his chest. "I must go," she said. "I have a long drive ahead of me."

He hopped down from the shelf-like arrangement formed by the straps suspended from the roof of the vehicle and the canvas stretcher. He tossed her clothes to her and scrambled into his. When she was ready he lifted her down. They crawled into the front seat and she started the engine.

"Can you find your way back all right?" he asked as they turned into the deeply rutted road back to the area. It had the makings of a nice day, puffy cumulus clouds played tag with the sun and the roar of engines warming-up told Macon that the urgent business of war was to consume much of his immediate attention. "Can you remember the way, Angel?"

"I think so," she said. "It won't be too hard during the day."

"Can you get away during the week?" he said. He lit them each a cigarette; she decline hers. "Not before breakfast," she said.

From behind the comforting smoke he drank in a long drink of the day. The sun looked as though it might shine, the clouds were being jostled right along by the impatient breeze that danced quickly through the area on tip-toe. The rain having stopped, the mud had lost its strongarmed ally and now looked neglected as it swished under the churning tires of the ambulance. "As soon as I can get an idea as to when I can expect to fly, I'll call you."

"Will you be able to come down to Naha?" she said.

"I doubt it; but I will certainly try," he said. "I hope I can wrangle a jeep. Do you think we can find someplace in Naha to go and celebrate in the proper manner?"

She laughed. "There must be someplace. However, the town isn't in very good shape."

"Forget it, Angel," he laughed. "I don't mean that kind of celebration."

She just looked at him for a moment, then looked away.

"I know exactly what you're thinking," he said. "Here I am just finished with one meal and already looking forward to the next. Well, maybe so—but aren't you complimented? Really, I would like to smuggle you into the Squadron, keep you right along side of me all the time—for luck."

She didn't say anything, she seemed to be having her hands full with the driving. At least she made sure that it would look that way.

"Listen, Angel; in case I can't get transportation, can you get this wagon again?"

"I don't know, Rush," she said. "I don't like the idea of coming up here like this."

"But, do you think you can get this boat again?" he said. "If it's the only transportation that we've got, it beats walking."

"I suppose I can—I don't know," she said. "Miss Watkins will probably be sore at me for keeping it out all night. She'll probably be sore at me period."

"Is she your guardian?"

"No, my friend."

"Well, I'll tell you what—you get the ambulance and I'll get down to your place and you can pick me up there."

"From no vehicle to two vehicles," she said. She thought it over for a moment. "Do we *need* the ambulance?"

"Let's have it though."

"I don't like the idea at all." The ambulance came to a slithering halt in front of the orderly room. He hopped out. "I don't like the idea at all," she said.

"I'll call you tomorrow or Tuesday, Angel. 'Bye." He slammed the door.

She nodded, shifted the gears, started to move off. He watched the vehicle crawl angrily through the deep road, then he crossed the street, climbed the bank, entered the tent. It was fifteen mintues before seven o'clock and neither Weaver nor Lloyd appeared to be alive. Macon stripped to his shorts, got into bed.

He awoke at eleven o'clock. The sun was in his eyes. He got dressed, washed, went to dinner. Weaver was in the tent when he returned.

"Well," Weaver said, "glad to see you."

"Hi."

"You must have had a large evening last night," Weaver said. "You didn't look very chipper when you came in this morning."

"So?"

"Nothing," Weaver said, almost apologetically. "I was just interested in seeing that you had fun."

"It was enjoyable, thank you. And yours?"

"Quiet, very quiet."

"Where is everybody. The place looks deserted." It seemed to Macon that he had been away from the area for years—its seemed as though he had been on a long leave, he felt practically like a visitor here. The one night away had been such an exciting change.

"Oh," Weaver said. "They came around at five this morning getting crews up for a mission. It seems they've spotted some shipping off Korea. It's lucky you weren't scheduled."

"Did Lloyd go?"

"No, but the clear weather made him feel ambitious, so he got himself a dinner "K" ration and went out for a hike."

"He would bear watching. This combat must be getting the best of him."

"No, he seemed okay," Weaver said, seriously. "He said he was restless. He should be back soon. He left at about eight and said he'd be back early this afternoon."

"So the boys went out on a strike. . . ."

"Yeah, six ships from each squadron." Weaver began to pace the floor. "I wish the hell they would send me out on a mission. This waiting around is driving me buggy."

"Why don't you stop racing your engine, you're wearing me down." Macon sat down on his cot, lit a cigarette. "Knocking yourself out like you do won't help things at all. You should know that by now."

"I can't help it."

"Well, you've just got to relax, that's all," Macon said. "Or you'll have us all nutty. It's just that the weather has been so stinking lately. We'll probably fly a lot now for a while—you'll have your day. Maybe then, you'll wish you weren't so eager."

"I know, I know. It's just that I don't know what to expect. I know that a week before I got here some guy in the Squadron went down on his first mission. In the ETO they say that the first mission is a jinx misison. You know, it's natural to sweat out the first one."

"Hell, sweat it out all you want to, if it'll make you feel better. I don't want to spoil your fun, but I wish you'd stop perspiring all over me."

"Didn't you sweat out your first strike?" Weaver said, impatiently. "Or did you start in on number two?"

"It was so long ago, I don't remember. And that's

when it was really rough. Now you could go indefinitely without ever seeing a Jap fighter. I've just about forgotten what they look like."

"I forgot," Weaver said quickly. "I forgot that you shouldn't start a conversation with the war heroes about their experiences; they want to forget, or something like that."

"Oh, forget it," Macon said. "You'll get past your missions okay. Relax, take it easy; you may even be surprised—you may even enjoy them."

"You know I think you do enjoy them."

"No; I wouldn't say that. I'll explain it to you sometime; when we're both drunk."

"Hmmmmm."

Macon lit a cigarette from the glow of the spent one. He tossed the stub away. He unlaced his shoes and kicked them off, lay down on the cot with hands folded behind his head. He studied the trail of the smoke from his cigarette as it built up and then suddenly blew away.

"Are you married, Weaver?"

"Nope."

"Got a girl?"

"Nope."

"What's the matter with you?"

"What's my marital status got to do with anything?"

"Nothing," Macon said. "Not a thing. I was just making conversation, that's all." He turned over as if to go to sleep, spotted Lloyd coming in.

"Well, how do you do," Lloyd said.

"Fine," Macon said. "How do *you* do?" Macon boosted himself up to an elbow. "I understand that you're considering getting transferred to the infantry; is that right?"

"No, the Chemical Warfare Service. Why?"

"Where did you walk to?" Weaver said.

"Oh, I went down to China, over to Bolo Point, around by the 82nd Seabees, and back. It was real nice. Not too far, just nice."

"I wish I had gone with you," Weaver said. "This sitting around doing nothing is getting me down."

"You talk like a man who doesn't sleep well at night," Macon said. "You've never killed anybody, have you?"

"No," Weaver said. "I haven't killed anybody yet. But I still don't sleep well."

"I can't understand it," Macon said. "You've got Buck's air mattress; it's one of the best in the Squadron. It doesn't leak at all. Buck never used to fill it more than once a week; maybe not even then."

"I guess you wouldn't understand even if he did tell you," Lloyd said.

"Why," Macon said, "is there something I should know that you jokers haven't told me about?"

"Heaven forbid," Lloyd said.

"How many combat points have you got, Lloyd?" Macon said. "I think this war is getting you too. You're beginning to take it too seriously."

"Perhaps, but I've still got more combat points than you have."

"Say," Weaver said suddenly, "how do those combat points work, anyway?"

"Well," Lloyd began, "you get three points for every ten combat hours. That comes to one point for every three hours and twenty minutes. You get one point for someone in your Squadron getting holed by enemy fire. You get two points if the Squadron loses an airplane over the target; if you get enemy interception and you have fighter cover, you get one point. If you get enemy interception and you don't have fighter cover, you get three points."

"And if you ditch," Macon said, "that's five points."

"I guess that's about all there is to it," Lloyd said.

"I think I'd just as soon fly out my combat hours for my points," Weaver said. "You need a hundred points to go back to the States, don't you?"

"Roger," Macon said. "That is roger."

"How many points have you guys got?" Weaver said. "I know you've been here for quite a while."

"Does it show?" Macon said.

"I have 69," Lloyd said. "He's got 65."

"When did you come over?"

"I came over during the first week in February," Lloyd said. "Macon got into the Squadron two weeks after I did."

"What kind of equipment do they give you when you go out on a mission?" Weaver said.

"What do you mean?" Lloyd said. "Guns, knives, first-aid kits, ammo, canteen, rations. . . ."

"No, I mean personal equipment in case you have to leave the plane."

"If you ever do, what you so coyly refer to as 'leaving the plane,' you really don't have much to worry about," Macon said, with a broad grin. "You probably will have augered in. When you're tooling along at about 300 miles per hour and are at 15 feet altitude things usually happen too fast to worry about."

"That's partly true," Lloyd said. "But in case you ditch or do get a chance to get out, they give you a 'Pointie-Talkie' book, with Chinese phrases and

English phrases that coincide in meaning. You look up a question that you want to ask some Chink you happen to meet and on the opposite page is the same question written in Chinese so that he can look right across and understand you. It's quite a gadget. Then, when you want some information you get him to point to a sentence in Chinese and the translation is opposite, there for you. It's really handy."

"They give you a waterproof map, too," Macon said. "It's really a shrewd item."

"Let's see," Lloyd said, as though he was thinking aloud. "They give you an American flag with writing underneath it in six different languages explaining that you are friendly, that you are an American—and, oh, yes—there's money. They give you a sealed packet of Chinese money that you can break open and use if necessary. Nothing goes quite as far as money in this part of the world."

"They're getting quite westernized," Macon said.

"The packet of money is sealed and you turn it back in after each mission. There are a limited number of them." Lloyd thought for a moment. "That's about all we get; isn't it, Make?" Macon nodded. "Of course, you have flak suits and helmets and rations and Mae Wests, and parachutes, beside the stuff you wear," Lloyd said.

"What do you fellows wear on a strike?" Weaver asked.

"I just wear a regular summer gabardine flying coverall suit," Lloyd said. "With G.I. high-top shoes and my personal equipment."

"This sounds like an old lady's fashion show," Macon said.

"The guy's just trying to find out some information," Lloyd said. "Go ahead, Don Juan, tell him about your natty outfit."

"I go resplendent in khakis," Macon said. "They're luxuriously cool and don't pinch, grab, or crowd."

"Everybody wears the regular high-top G.I. shoes, don't they?" Weaver said.

"Yeah, but don't tell the infantry," Macon said. "They're sure we wear black-and-white pumps; I would hate to disillusion them."

"Yes, indeed," Lloyd said, ignoring Macon, "if you ever have to walk back it's hard to hike in bare feet, because you'll lose those low-cut jobs if you bail out. The shock of the 'chute opening will snap low shoes right off your feet."

"How about practice flying?" Weaver said. "Will I fly practice missions, or go right out?"

"There's no set rule," Lloyd said. "It depends on the situation and how badly they need you." He glanced at his watch. "I've got to go over to operations," he said. "I'll see you later." He went out.

Weaver lit a cigarette, stood in the center of the floor, eyeing his equipment with the keenness of a customer about to make a purchase. He smoked the cigarette quickly, exhaling a thick cloud of smoke.

"You're making it look like Joe's Pool Hall in here," Macon said.

Weaver ignored him. He walked over to his B-4 bag, delved down into its innards, produced his .45 pistol. "Don't shoot," Macon laughed. "I was only kidding."

The humor went unappreciated. Weaver was studying the weapon. "Is there any place around

here where you can practice shooting the .45?"
Weaver said.

"Not that I know of; why?"

"Oh, I dunno. . . ."

"It's a good idea though," Macon said. "Damn
good idea." He felt like he had hit on some
entertaining diversion.

"Do you really think so?"

"You damn-well betcha' I do," Macon said,
holding himself in check with what he concluded
must be masterful self-control. "No telling when
you'll have to shoot—and make the shots count."

"Well, I'd like to get sharp with this gun; just in
case I *do* have to use it sometime."

"Keep it in good shape; that's the secret," Macon
said. "Buck had some equipment for cleaning and
oiling the gun. He had all that stuff. Look over
there in his box; I think it's still there. . . ."

Weaver looked, found, fingered, fondled, forgot
that Macon was watching. Macon sang encouragement. "That oil evaporates pretty quickly; I imagine
it'll be gone soon in this windy, sunny weather."

He said no more; nothing else was necessary.
Having planted the seed, Macon relaxed on his cot,
arms crossed behind his head, as a pillow, feet
wooing each other; a newly-lighted cigarette for
company. Weaver was already furiously at work.
He had his pistol stripped and was working intently
on the scattered parts.